# SIX TREES

See p. 87

"'WHERE IS MY WIFE?'"

# SIX TREES

Short Stories

By
MARY ELEANOR WILKINS FREEMAN

Short Story Index Reprint Series

BOOKS FOR LIBRARIES PRESS
FREEPORT, NEW YORK

First Published 1903
Reprinted 1969


STANDARD BOOK NUMBER:
8369-3100-9

LIBRARY OF CONGRESS CATALOG CARD NUMBER:
74-94721

MANUFACTURED
BY
HALLMARK LITHOGRAPHERS, INC.
IN THE U.S.A.

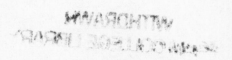

# CONTENTS

# ILLUSTRATIONS

# ILLUSTRATIONS

# The
# ELM-TREE

# THE ELM-TREE

THE elm-tree had his field to himself. He stood alone in a wide and deep expanse of wind-swept grass which once a year surged round him in foaming billows crested with the rose of clover and the whiteness of daisies and the gold of buttercups. The rest of the time the field was green with an even slant of lush grass, or else it was a dun surface, or else a glittering level of snow; but always there stood the tree, with his green branches in the summer, his gold ones in the autumn, his tender,

gold-green ones in the spring, and his
branches of naked grace in the winter,
but always he was superb.  There was
not in the whole country-side another
tree which could compare with him.  He
was matchless.  Never a stranger passed
the elm but stopped and stared and
said something or thought something
about it.  Even dull rustics looked, and
had a momentary lapse from vacuity.
The tree was compelling.  He insisted
upon a recognition of his beauty and
grace.  Let one try to pass him unheed-
ing and sunken in the contemplation of
his own little affairs, and, lo! he would
force himself out of the landscape not
only upon the eyes, but the very soul,
which, turned away from self, would see
the tree through its windows, like a rev-
elation and proof of that which is outside and beyond.  It became at such

times, to some minds, something akin to a testimony of God. Something there was about the superb acres of those great branches curving skyward and earthward with matchless symmetry of line which seemed to furnish an upward lift for thought and imagination. The field in which the tree stood was a great parallelogram. On the left-hand side, across a stone wall, was a house almost as old as the tree. On the other side, across a new, painted fence, was a modern house, pretentious and ornate with bracketed cornices, bay-windows, a piazza, and a cupola. This cupola especially disturbed the mind of the dweller in the old house. The name of this dweller was David Ransom. He was quite old, and had a stiff leg which necessitated a gait wherein one limb described a rigid half-circle before it was brought to the accomplishment of a forward step. He had been incapacitated from work for some years. All he had in the world was his poor ancient house and an acre of land in the rear on which he raised vegetables and kept a few hens which furnished his humble sustenance. Once it had been very different. He had owned the great field on which the elm stood; he had even owned the new house beyond, although in a simpler form. He had built it very largely with his own hands, for, though ostensibly a farmer, he had been a Jack of all trades, and able to turn his hand to almost any craft with skill. He had lived in the old Ransom house, which had been in the family for four generations, until he was almost an old man and his wife an old woman; then with the pitiful savings of a lifetime he had built the new one. He

"CURVING SKYWARD AND EARTHWARD WITH MATCHLESS
SYMMETRY"

had loved and handled tenderly every nail he had put into it, every fragrant length of pine; he had built it with the utmost that was in him. Then, just as it was finished, he had lost it. The bank in which his savings were stored had failed, and there was nothing to meet the payments for the stock. He sold the house and the field at a miserable sacrifice, and used the proceeds to pay the bills, all except a proportion which he was obliged to work out. The old wife died shortly afterwards; the disappointment had been too much for her. All her life she had planned and dreamed about the new house which was to stand on the vacant lot. She had thought about it until in a sense she had really lived in it, and an actual building had tumbled about her ears.

After she died, David lived alone, and

wound himself up like a caterpillar in a cocoon of repining and misanthropy. He seemed bitter to the core. He was in spirit a revolutionist and anarchist. The mention of banks sent him into a white heat of rage. He nursed his grievances until they turned upon himself and stung him to his own spiritual harm. One of his special bitternesses was the improvements which the new owner had made in his new house. He resented them as he might have done any pointing out of his own personal defects. When the new owner, whose name was Thomas Savage, set about building the bay-window on the blank of the south wall, David fairly swelled with indignation and humiliation. That morning he went across the road and unbottled his wrath to old Abner Slocum. Old Abner lived with his daughter, who was a dressmaker—it was an unskilful, desultory sort of dress-making at very low prices—and thereby supported in frugal comfort herself and her father, who was very deaf. Old Abner, on pleasant days in warm weather, spent most of his time on the porch, for his room was better than his company in the sitting-room, which was also the apartment used for fitting dresses. David Ransom spent many an hour with him, seated on the top step of the porch. Abner had an old kitchen chair tipped back against the house wall. On that morning when the scaffolding for the new bay-window was erected David went across the street swinging his lame leg around viciously. That was the second spring after the rheumatism had attacked him. It was a hot, moist morning in early May. The trees were beginning to cast leaf-shadows, and the air was cloyed with sweet. Old Abner, on the porch, was in his shirt-sleeves, his feet were covered with great carpet slippers. He grinned vacuously as David approached. A curtain of a window behind him went down with a snap, shutting out a glimpse of a young woman upon whom his daughter was about to try a new gown.

Abner did not hear it, but he felt it, and he smiled slyly at the new-comer. "Mari's tryin' on a new gownd to the Ames gal," he chuckled.

David nodded with impatient scorn. The curtain might as well have been lowered for a shadow as for him. He settled himself laboriously on the porch step in front of Abner. His lame leg was stretched out unbendingly into Maria Slocum's bed of lady's-delights, which came up faithfully in their old place every spring. David ground his heel viciously down among the flowers. He scowled at Abner with almost malignity. He jerked a shoulder towards the right. "Seen what they are doin' over there?" he inquired, gruffly.

Old Abner did not hear him. He had been gazing forth at the glories of the spring morning, and he answered from the fulness of his thought.

"Yes, I guess spring is 'most here, sure 'nough," he said, happily. He made a curious nestling motion with his old shoulders in a warm sunbeam which lay over them like a caressing arm. He smiled contentedly. Now were come for him the long days of peaceful dozing on the porch, undisturbed by his daughter's dress-making, the days of plenty of garden greens and vegetables and fruit. Keenly sensitive to material sweets was old Abner Slocum.

But David Ransom sniffed with fury. "Spring!" he cried. Then he shouted, reaching out a knotted hand and clutching the other's lean shank with a fierce grip. He gesticulated violently towards the house on which the workmen were hammering. "See what they're doin' of over there?" he demanded, biting off every word and syllable shortly; and old Abner heard, or, if he did not hear, grasped the meaning of the pointing hand and the smart grip on his leg.

"Yes," he answered, cheerfully, "makin' improvements, ain't they?"

"Improvements!" shrieked David Ransom — "improvements! improvements! When that house was fit for the President to live in before. Improvements! Good Lord!"

"That winder is goin' to look real pooty, ain't it?" inquired old Abner, innocently.

David glared. He rose, dragging his lame leg after him. "Be you a fool?" he shouted. Then he was gone down the path with his stiff strut, while old Abner gazed after him, amiably open-mouthed like a baby. Presently he began to nod, and finally fell asleep in the moist light, with his head sunken on his breast.

But David Ransom sat alone on the doorstep of his old house, and all day long his regard never left the carpenters working on the new one across the field. When the bay-window and the new piazza were completed, and the tin roofs glittered in the sun, David fell fairly ill. He neither ate nor slept. His eyes looked wild in their jungle of unkempt beard

13

and long, white hair. He talked to himself a good deal; he made furious gestures when walking. Children turned to stare after him; once in a while they ran away when they saw him coming. There began to be talk of taking care of him, sending him somewhere to be looked out for, lest he do harm to himself and others. His old house and land might pay his board for the rest of his life, for he seemed feeble.

David knew nothing of this. He continued to inveigh with a rancor which had the force of malignity at the improvements on the new house. When at last the cupola was built, that was the climax. When Maria Slocum saw him coming across the road to talk it over with her father, she hustled the old man into the house. "David Ransom is clean out of his head," she said, "and I ain't goin' to have him comin' over here. I'm afraid of him."

So when David reached the Slocum house he found the door bolted and the window - curtain down, with cautious gaps for peering at the sides, for Maria, her father, and a woman whom she was fitting, but David did not see them. He went stiffly home, talking all the way so loudly that they could hear what he said. " Bad enough to hev it in the fust place, then to go and build on to it winders and piazzers and cupolys, as if it wa'n't good enough for him. Guess what was good enough for Sarah an' me was good enough for him." Then he finished with a refrain of misery, " Winders, piazzers, cupolys, new stun steps, and a new tin ruff." He said the last in a sort of singsong over and over. That was the burden of his

thoughts, the summing up of his grievances.

"Something had ought to be done
about David Ransom," said Maria Slocum to the woman who was being fitted,
and the woman agreed with her.

That night a strange thing happened:
one of the catastrophes which serve to
punctuate and paragraph the monotony
of village life. The new house which
had been built by David Ransom and
purchased and improved by Thomas
Savage was burned to the ground. At
midnight the sky was rosy for miles
around, and the air resonant with bells;
at dawn there was only a bed of glowing
coals and ashes. Everybody, of course,
suspected David, although there was no
proof except his well-known bitterness
regarding the improvements. He was
under a ban, though he was not arrested.

"'WINDERS, PIAZZERS, CUPOLYS, NEW STUN STEPS, AND A NEW TIN RUFF'"

It was decided that he was a dangerous character, in spite of his age and feebleness, and ought not to be at such entire liberty to work out his own devices, and that, moreover, he ought, humanly speaking, to be cared for comfortably.

One afternoon old Abner Slocum, sitting on the front porch with a handkerchief over his face to keep the flies off, and presumably dozing, heard his daughter Maria tell the woman whom she was fitting that David was to be carried the next day to Eleazer Wise's to board. Eleazer and his wife had occasionally taken old people, whom no one else wanted to board, for a small consideration. "The town has took it up," said Maria.

"You don't say so," said the woman, turning sidewise to look at the fit of her bodice. "Ain't there a little pouch where the sleeve goes in?"

"That 'll be all right when it's stitched. They don't think it's safe for him to be 'round, and they don't think he has proper victuals. For my part, I ain't afraid of him as I used to be before the house was burned. He don't talk to himself, nor make motions the way he used to. He just sits real kind of still on his doorstep. He come over here to see father the other day, and he seemed real mild and gentle. I ain't a mite afraid of him, nor I ain't afraid he'll set me afire, and I never believed he set Thomas Savage afire. Mis' Savage was always dreadful careless about fire—used to carry live coals in a shovel all over the house when she wanted to kindle fires in the air-tight stoves, and the Savage boy made a bonfire in the barn once. They

18

don't tell of it, on account of the insurance, but I heard it real straight; and they ain't goin' to build there again; goin' out of town; guess there's reason enough. I ain't goin' to believe that David Ransom did such a thing as that, if he did used to talk so. He's had an awful hard time, and it wa'n't his fault."

"S'pose he'll take it hard goin' to 'Leazer's," said the woman.

"I'm dreadful afraid he will, and I don't blame him. I know 'Leazer Wise, and his wife, too. I know how I'd feel if it was father goin'."

"Your father 'll feel bad to have him go."

"Yes; I 'ain't dared say anything about it to father."

A little later Maria, glancing out of the window, after taking in an underarm seam, exclaimed, "Why, where's father?"

"Ain't he there?" asked the woman, screwing her head around.

"No, and he was sittin' there just a minute ago, sound asleep. Well, mebbe the flies plagued him, and he's gone down in the orchard under the trees; sometimes he does."

Old Abner Slocum had just toddled out of sight around the Ransom house opposite, to the garden where David was picking some corn for his supper. A little later he returned, and his daughter saw him. She came to the door, the woman's dress - waist in her hand. "Where have you been, father?" she cried, drawing her thread through.

Old Abner did not hear, but he knew what she said. "Over to David's," he replied, quaveringly. His eyes looked watery and his mouth unusually firm.

Maria regarded him sharply. Then she reflected that he must have been asleep, and not able to hear, in any case, what she and the woman had been talking about.

"Well, you'd better sit down and keep cool, father," said she; "you look all het up."

Then she re-entered the house, and old Abner settled himself in his chair on the porch. Presently one of the selectmen of the village, who lived a little farther down the road, and who was to take David to Eleazer Wise's next morning, rode by in a light express-wagon in a cloud of dust. "Hullo, Abner! Hot day!" he shouted, urbanely. Abner waited until he had passed, then he slowly shook his fist at him.

The next morning Maria Slocum kept down the curtain of her front window facing the Ransom house. "I dun'no' as you can see in here," she said to her first customer, "but they are goin' to take David Ransom to board to 'Leazer Wise's this morning; they think he ought to be looked after, and I don't want to see it. He's lived there ever since I was born, and father sets a heap by him, and he's had a hard time, poor man. I don't see why they can't let him alone. He never set that fire any more than I did, and he wouldn't hurt a baby kitten; never would, for all he used to talk so. If he ain't quite so comfortable where he is, he's enough sight happier than he'll be to 'Leazer's."

"I've heard 'Leazer Wise wa'n't any too mild," said the other woman.

# THE ELM-TREE

"I wouldn't want *father* to go there," said Maria.

There was a sound of wheels outside. "Guess 'Leazer and John Dagget have come for him now," said Maria.

The woman peeped round the curtain. "Yes, they hev," said she; "it's John's wagon."

"They're goin' to try to let the house, and have the rent pay his board," said Maria. "See anything of him?"

"No. They're just goin' in the front gate. Now they're knockin'."

"Anybody come to the door?"

"No. They're knocking again."

"Anybody come?"

"No. Now they're tryin' the door."

"Are they goin' in?"

"Yes, they're goin' in."

There was a silence. Presently Maria spoke. "See anything of him?"

"No; can't see a sign of anybody."

"Ain't it dreadful queer?"

"Seems to me it is. You don't s'pose anything has happened, do you?"

"I dun'no'. It's dreadful queer."

The woman made an exclamation.

"What is it?" asked Maria, anxiously. "What do you see, Mis' Abbot?"

"Why, they're comin' out," replied the woman.

"He with 'em?"

"No, he ain't. My land!"

"What is it?"

"They're comin' over here."

Indeed, as she spoke Eleazer Wise and the selectman crossed the road to the Slocum house, and Maria ran trembling to the door.

The woman who was being fitted stood back out of sight, since she had not her dress on, and listened at the

24

door. She heard Maria reply to a question in her high, agitated voice. " No, David Ransom ain't here. I 'ain't set eyes on him to-day. You can't find him? You don't say so! What do you s'pose has happened to him?"

Old Abner Slocum sat on the porch, with his handkerchief over his eyes. He had not stirred. Maria shook him violently by the shoulder, as Eleazer Wise inquired of him if he had seen David Ransom that day, and his voice was strained to razor - like sharpness, though it was naturally soft. But old Abner did not hear. He gave a sleepy grunt like a disturbed animal, shrugged his shoulder loose from his daughter's grasp, flirted the handkerchief pettishly over his face, settled his head back, and gave vent to an ostentatious snore.

Eleazer Wise, who was a thin-nosed,

pensive-looking man, and the selectman, who was exceedingly tall and bore himself with a dull dignity, went their ways in the latter's light wagon, presumably to search for David Ransom. The horse was whipped to a smart trot. Maria called after them to know what they were going to do, but she got no response. She looked hard at her father, who sat quite still, making a loud, purring sound. Then she went into the house. The minute she was gone old Abner slipped the handkerchief from his face, and stared with a wonderful keenness of bright old eyes across the road at the beautiful elm-tree in the midst of the field in a rosy and green foam of grass and clover. He waved the handkerchief which he had taken from his face. There was a tiny answering gleam of white from the massy greenness of the elm. Old Abner chuckled softly. Then he muttered to himself, "Can't do nothin' afore dark," and settled for a nap in good faith.

It was a very warm night, and dark except for the stars. The twilight lingered long, but at last the village lay in deep shadow, and one could not distinguish objects far in advance. Once that night Maria Slocum thought she heard a noise on the porch, and got out of bed and thrust her head out of the open window. "Anybody there?" she called, softly and timorously. There was a dead silence. She peered into the darkness, but could see nothing. She went back to bed, and thought she must have been mistaken. Once after that she was wakened from sleep by a strange sound, and this time she light-

ed a candle and crossed the little entry
to her father's room. She opened the
door softly, and a glance showed her
the gleam of the white head on the pil-
low.

"Must have been rats," she thought,
and returned to her own chamber, and
slept undisturbed the rest of the night.

The next morning she went into the
pantry to cut some slices from a piece
of corned beef, and stared incredulous-
ly. She looked everywhere, standing
on tiptoe to search the upper shelves.
Then she hurried into the kitchen,
where her father sat waiting for his
breakfast. He cast a scared glance at
her as she entered; then he turned his
chair around with a grating noise and
stared intently out of the window.
"Well, you've got to go without your
breakfast," said Maria.

# THE ELM-TREE

Old Abner made no sign.

Maria raised her voice higher. "Can't you hear, father?" she cried. "You'll have to go without your breakfast. There ain't a thing in the house to eat but some bread-and-butter."

The old man rolled one bright eye at her over his shoulder, then he stared out of the window again. A red flush was evident mounting his neck to his thin fringe of white hair.

"All that corn' beef is gone, every mite of it," proclaimed Maria, in a voice of tragedy. "I heard a noise last night. I knew I did. There was a thief in this house last night, father."

Old Abner appeared to hear. His shoulders heaved, but he did not look around.

"A thief came into this house through the pantry window, and stole all that corn' beef," repeated Maria. "It's gone, and it couldn't go without hands. Some tramp, I s'pose, that was hungry. I paid 'most fifty cents for that corn' beef, but I s'pose I ought to be thankful. He might have stole Miss Bemis's black silk dress. You'll have to put up with toasted bread for your breakfast, father. Do you hear, father? You'll have to put up with toasted bread and coffee for your breakfast."

"All right," mumbled the old man.

Maria went out of the room, and the sound of the coffee-mill in the shed resounded through the house. Then old Abner turned around and noiselessly doubled himself up with merriment.

The day was very pleasant and clear, although still warm. Maria toiled at her dress - making, and old Abner sat peacefully on the porch. The selectman and Eleazer visited the house once, and inquired if they had seen anything of David; they also searched again in the old Ransom house. In the afternoon, just after the two men had driven away, and Maria had the front curtains drawn to keep out the sun, old Abner stole around the house, got a tin pail from the pantry, drew it full of cold water at the well, and slunk swiftly, padding like an old dog in his carpet - slippered feet, across the opposite field to the elm-tree.

He stood underneath, casting wary glances around; he held the pail, catching a gleam of the western sun from its polished sides until it looked as if on fire. He fumbled away at its handle, then suddenly, as if by some unseen agency, it was drawn up and out of sight into the green umbrage of the great tree. Old Abner turned about gleefully after

a furtive hiss of whisper sent after the
ascending pail, and his daughter Maria
stood unexpectedly behind him. Sly-
ness and sharpness were family traits.
She had been suspicious ever since she
had missed the meat in the morning.
Old Abner turned quite pale. He
chuckled feebly to hide his consterna-
tion, and he stared helplessly at Maria.

"What in creation are you doing
here, father?" she asked, sternly. She
spoke quite low, but he heard her perfectly.

"I ain't doin' anything, Mari," he replied, feebly, shifting in his carpet slippers.

"You needn't talk that way to me,
father; I know better. You're up to
something. What were you doing with
that pail, and how came it to go up in
the tree?"

Maria peered upward, and stood transfixed. Out of the great spread of the tree, that majesty of green radiances and violet shadows and high-lights as of emeralds—out of this fairy mottle, as of jewels and shadows and sunbeams, stared the face of old David Ransom, and the face was inexpressibly changed. All the bitterness and rancor were gone.

It was the face of a man in shelter from the woes and stress of life. He looked forth from the beautiful arms of the great tree as a child from the arms of its mother. He had fled for shelter to a heart of nature, and it had not failed him. He smiled down at Maria with a peaceful triumph.

"They never thought of lookin' for me here," he called down. "I wa'n't goin' to 'Leazer's."

"David Ransom, you 'ain't been up

33

there all this time, in that tree!" gasped Maria. "Why, they've got men huntin' in the woods, and they're goin' to drag the pond."

David laughed in a silver strain as sweetly as a child.

"Never thought of lookin' for me here," said he. "I wa'n't goin' to 'Leazer's."

"How on earth did you ever get up there with your lame leg?"

"I clim."

"How? You wa'n't up there all night?"

David nodded, setting the green leaves nodding. He was comfortably astride a large bough, with another below it, affording him a rest for his feet. His back and head were against the trunk of the tree. He rested as comfortably as if in an arm-chair midway of the tree, entirely concealed from view except to one standing directly beneath him.

"It beats all," said Maria. "I s'pose you carried him that corn' beef, father? That was where it went to."

"I wa'n't goin' to let an old neighbor starve, Mari," said old Abner, with boldness.

Maria stood staring at him.

"I carried him some bread, too, an' a piece of squash pie," said old Abner, defiantly, in his cracked treble of age.

Maria looked up at old David in the tree. "Mr. Ransom, you come down here as quick as you can," said she, authoritatively.

David made an attempt to climb higher. His bough rocked.

"Come right down here," repeated Maria. "You 'ain't got to go to

'Leazer's. I ain't afraid of you. You didn't set that house afire, did you?"

"No, I didn't," called down David.

"Well, you come down here. You sha'n't go to 'Leazer's. You can board with me. I need the money as much as 'Leazer Wise. You can have the south chamber, or you can sleep in your own house, if you want to, till it's rented, if you'd feel more to home."

"I've moved out of my old house," called David.

"All right, you can have the south chamber in my house, and you and father can have real good times together. Come down. Can you git down?"

David began swinging himself downward with painful slowness.

"Be careful you don't fall and break your bones."

36

# THE ELM-TREE

David descended. When he was just ready to slide down the shaggy trunk below the spread of large branches, he paused and looked down at Maria with lingering doubt and distrust.

"You needn't be afraid," said Maria. The tears were running down her cheeks. "You sha'n't go anywheres you don't want to. I'll look out for you, and I'd like to see anybody stop me." There was decision in Maria's voice which compelled confidence. Still, David looked down hesitatingly, like a child afraid to leave its mother.

"Come right along," said Maria, "and look out you don't fall and break your bones. I've got some nice griddle-cakes for supper and a custard pie."

David slid down.

After that the two old men could

have been seen all day seated on the porch of the Slocum house wrapped in the silence of peaceful memories. A family moved into the old Ransom house, and they enjoyed watching the children play about. David took a fancy to one little girl. Sometimes he coaxed her over, and he told her one story of his own childhood which his father had told him. It was uncouth and pointless, but the child loved it, and the two men hailed its climax always with innocent laughter. The three were children together. Old David was never bitter nor rebellious in those days, but his mind was somewhat affected after a curious and, as some would have it, merciful fashion. Maria said openly that it was a blessing that he looked at things the way he did, that she believed that the Lord was

"'I'VE GOT SOME NICE GRIDDLE-CAKES FOR SUPPER
AND A CUSTARD PIE'"

sort of tellin' him stories to keep him goin' in his hard road of life, the way folks tell stories to children. She discovered it before old David had been domiciled with her twenty-four hours.

It was the next morning after he came there. He and her father were talking together on the porch, and she heard David saying this to old Abner: "You see that house over there," said he; "ain't it handsome? It's the handsomest house in this town, and it's all mine. Nobody else has the right to set foot in it. I had it painted green, and it's higher than the meetin'-house. Can't nobody find any fault with that house. Nobody is going to build cupolys nor bay-winders on that, I can tell ye. It's jest right."

Maria and the woman whom she was fitting stared at each other.

"Did you hear that?" asked Maria, pale and trembling.

"He's out of his head," said the woman.

Maria leaned out of the window. "Where is your house, Mr. Ransom?" she asked, in a gentle voice.

Old David pointed.

"He means the elm - tree," said Maria.

The
WHITE BIRCH

# THE WHITE BIRCH

T one time the birch-tree had sisters, and they stood close together in sun and wind and rain, in winter and summer. Their pretty, graceful limbs were intertwined; their rustling leaves were so intermingled that one could not tell to which they belonged; the same rain fell on all alike; the same snows bent them to the ground in long garlands of grace; the same misty winds lashed them about; the same sunlight awoke their green leaves like green butterflies in the spring. But all her sisters were

gone; one or two had died of themselves, the others had been lopped
down by the woodsman, and there was
only the one white birch left. She
stood with the same inclination of her
graceful trunk and limbs which she
had had on account of her sisters, and
which she never would have had except for them. She was a tree alone,
but with the habit of one growing in
the midst of a family. All her lines
and motions were leanings towards an
old love. The white birch felt always,
as a man will feel a missing limb, the
old spread of the others' branches, the
wind and the rain and the sun in them.
She never fairly knew that she was
alone, that her sisters were not there.
When the snows of winter fell, she felt
them, soft and cool and sheltering,
weighing down her sisters' limbs as well

as her own; when the spring rain came, there was not a young leaf of the trees which were gone but was evident to her consciousness; and when the birds returned and sang and nested, she was never sure that they were not in her sisters' green-draped arms instead of her own. But there were times when she had a bewildered feeling that something was wrong, that something was gone. She lived in a grove where there were many other birch-trees, most of them growing in clumps; and sometimes, looking at them, she had a sense of loss.

Not very far from the tree was Joseph Lynn's house, the old Lynn homestead where he had been born and had lived for fifty years. The house, from some idiosyncrasy of his ancestors, had been set back from the highway in the fields, close to the birch grove. The descendants had often wondered and rebelled at the will of the dead man who had built the house. They wondered if he had wished to turn the highway from its course, if he had had some old feud with a neighbor. There had been talk of moving the house, though it would have been a severe undertaking to move the square old structure, built of massive timbers around an enormous central chimney. But Joseph, who was the last of his race, never had contemplated the moving until recently. Perhaps there was in him something of the spirit of the ancestor who had set the homestead in its isolated place. He loved to be away from the windows of neighbors, and the rattle of wheels along the dusty road; he loved the silent companionship of trees and fields,

46

and had no wish for anything else until he fell in love with Sarah Benton. He would call her Sarah, even to his own thoughts, although she was Sadie to everybody else. There was in him, in spite of apparent pliability and gentleness, a vein of obstinacy, and he loved the old above the new. His own mother's name had been Sarah; he rejected the modern paraphrase of it. The girl herself was cheaply and inanely pretty; by some method known to love, and love alone, he was blind to that element of commonness and unworthiness, and saw only in her the woman of his dreams. He refined her to such an extent with the fires of his love that, had she seen herself as she existed in his mind, she would never have known herself. She had spent many hours before her looking-glass in

her short life, but she had never possessed a looking-glass like that.

People in the village said that Joseph
Lynn was a fool to marry such a pretty,
silly young thing at his age, and in the
same breath said that she was a girl
who knew how to feather her nest, and
yet condemned her for being willing to
give herself to a man old enough to be
her father. Nobody dreamed that she
loved him. The girl was poor. She went
about dress-making from house to house
to support herself; and Joseph had his
comfortable home, and income enough
to almost keep her in luxury, or what
meant luxury to a girl of her standing
in life. People looked at her with a
mixture of approval of her shrewdness
and contempt. One young girl mate
of hers attacked her openly. She
boarded with this girl's mother, and one

night after Joseph Lynn had been court-
ing, she spoke out.  She went into the
parlor and stood before Sarah, fairly
trembling with indignation and maidenly shame.  The girl was very plain, with
a face so severe in its maidenliness that
it seemed like a sharp wedge of accu-
sation.  She had never had a lover in
all her life; she never would have.  She
had never even dreamed of love.  She
lived her life and did her duty without
passion ; that which had brought her
into being seemed not to exist in her.
Her drab - colored hair was combed
straight back from her uncompromising outlook of face; her skin was
dull, and the blushes struggled through
it.  She held her two hands clinch-
ed at her sides ; her figure, wide
and flat-bosomed, looked as rigid as
iron.

"I want to know," said she, "if you are really going to marry him."

"Yes, I am," replied the other girl. Her pretty face blazed, she shrugged her shoulders, and looked down at the ruffle of her gown.

"Going to marry that man?" repeated the other girl.

"I'd like to know why I shouldn't. What is there the matter with him?" asked Sarah, defiantly.

"Marrying a man old enough to be your father for a home," said the girl.

"Lots of girls do."

"I don't see why that makes it any better for you. You can't care anything about him."

"I'd like to know what's the matter with him. He's a good, kind man."

"And he's got money," said the other girl, in a tone of ineffable contempt and shame, as if she were ashamed of herself as well as her friend. As she spoke she looked as if she saw Joseph Lynn standing before her, and Sarah Benton looked at the same place, as if she also saw him. Indeed, both girls saw him with their minds' eyes, standing before them as visibly as if he had been there in the flesh. They saw a very tall, stiffly carriaged man, with a disproportionately long neck, and a cloud of curly blond beard like moss, which reached well over his breast. He was not a man to appeal to the fancy of any young girl, but rather to repel her, and awaken her ridicule through a certain unnamable something which seemed to mark him as unmated with youth and youthful fancies.

"You ain't going to marry him?" said again the other girl, whose name was Maria. All the shame of maidenly imagination was in her voice and her look, and Sarah quailed before it.

"I'd like to know why not?" she demanded, but her voice faltered.

"Marry him?" repeated the girl. The two words meant everything. Sarah blushed hotly.

"He's a good, kind man," she half whimpered out—"a good, kind man, and I'm alone in the world, and he'll take care of me; and I've always worked hard, and—" Sarah began to sob convulsively.

"How about Harry Wyman?"

Sarah Benton only sobbed more unrestrainedly.

"Harry Wyman has only got his day's wages, and he lost his job, anyhow, last month; but you couldn't wait," said Maria. "And you know you like him best, and you know how he feels about you, and now you'll marry this other man; you'll sell yourself."

"Stop talking to me so!" cried Sarah, with a flash of resentment.

"I won't; it's the truth," said Maria, mercilessly. "You do mean to sell yourself." She drew herself up and looked at Sarah with an unspeakable scorn and contempt. "You mean to marry him," she repeated, and again there was all the meaning which the imagination of a maiden could put into her voice and words. Then she turned and went out. She heard Sarah's convulsive sobs as she went, but she felt pitiless. The sitting-room door was open and her mother was sewing by the lamp, with its flowered shade. Maria cast a glance at her, and knew that she would be questioned curiously, and opened the front door and went down the walk between the rows of flowering bushes—pinks and peonies and yellow lilies. The katydids were singing very loud and shrill across the way. Somehow she felt a sort of futile anger at the sound. The ceaseless reverberations of nature which pertained to its perpetuation irritated her. It was the voice of a law under which she would never come, which she did not in her heart recognize, which, when she saw it applied to others, filled her with impatience and repulsion.

When she reached the gate, she stood still, leaning against it, and a man's figure loomed up before her. She did not start; she was not a nervous girl; she looked intently and recognized him in a moment.

"Is it you, Harry?" she said, in a low voice.

The man came closer. "Yes," he said, with a sort of gasp. Then he leaned heavily against the gate, and put his head down upon it with a sort of despairing gesture like a child.

Maria stood watching him, not so much pityingly as angrily. She thought to herself how could any man make such a fool of himself over a girl like that in there.

But she waited, and presently spoke in a low, soft voice, that her mother might not hear. "What's the matter? Are you sick?"

"Tell me, Maria, is she going to marry Joseph Lynn?" gasped the young fellow, with an agonized roll of black eyes at her.

"So she says."

55

"I wish I was dead."

"It ain't right to talk so."

"You don't know how I feel," groaned the young man, and that was perfectly true. "I've just got a job, too," said he, "and I came down here, and I saw him going away, and I wish I was dead."

The gate opened inward. Maria began pulling at it. "Here, come in," said she.

"What use is there, when—"

"Come in," said Maria, imperatively, pulling at the gate.

The young man yielded. He followed Maria into the house. Sarah was still sobbing. They could hear her the moment they entered the front entry. Maria's mother had not noticed, because she was slightly deaf.

Maria took the young man by the

arm, and almost forced him into the parlor. "Here he is," said she, in a curious voice, almost as if she were a being of another race, and spoke from the outside of things. "Here is Harry Wyman, and he's got another job, and if you've got a mite of shame you'll marry him instead of Joseph Lynn, Sadie Benton."

Then she shut the parlor door and went into the sitting-room.

Her mother looked up with a start; she had shut the parlor door with a bang.

"Who's in there now?" she whispered.

"Harry Wyman."

"For the land's sake! Which is she goin' to marry?"

"I don't know. I don't see what any woman who is earning her own livin' wants to get married for, anyhow," said Maria. "You go to bed, mother, if you want to."

"Do you know how long he's goin' to stay?"

"No, but I'll sit up and lock the door."

"She'll never think of it, she's so heedless."

"I told you *I* would, mother."

Joseph Lynn had made all his preparations to move his house to the edge of the highway. Sarah had complained that it was too far from the road, that she wanted to see the passing. The very next morning men assembled with jacks and timbers loaded on a wagon, and the heavy old horse which had drawn them was taken out and tied to a tree which he tried to nibble, and the

men were about beginning their task
when Harry Wyman came. He looked
pale, both shamed and triumphant.
He went up to Joseph, who surveyed
him with a kindly air. He had known
the young fellow ever since he was a
baby. He had never been jealous of
him, although he had heard his name
coupled with his sweetheart's. He was
not a jealous man, and believed in a
promise as he believed in the return of
the spring.

"Hello, Harry!" he said. "Want a
job?"

"No, thank you; I've got one."

"Oh. I heard you were out of work,
and thought mebbe I could give you a
lift."

The young man stood before the elder
one, still with that mixture of triumph
and shame. He could not speak out

his errand at once. He hedged. "Goin'
to move the old house?" he said,
huskily.

"Yes; then I'm goin' to have her
painted up and shingled, and a bay-
winder put on, and get some new furni-
ture. Suppose you've heard I'm goin'
to be married?"

"Yes, I've heard," said the young
man. He turned perceptibly paler.

Joseph stared at him with sudden
concern. "What in creation ails you?"
he said. "Be you sick? Want anything to take?"

"No. Look here—"

Harry drew him aside and told him.
"She's liked me best all the time," he
said. "You won't be hard on her, Mr.
Lynn?"

Joseph's face was ghastly, but he lost
not one atom of his stiffness of bearing.

"'SUPPOSE YOU'VE HEARD I'M GOIN' TO BE MARRIED?'"

He was like a tree that even the winds of heaven could not bend. "If she likes you best, that's all there is to be said about it," he replied, and his voice, although it was quite steady, seemed to come from far away.

"I hope you won't lay it up against her. She's a little, delicate thing, and I'd lost my job, and—"

"If she likes you better, that's all there is to say about it," repeated Joseph, in a tone so hardly conclusive that the young fellow jumped.

He went away with a leaping motion of joy, in spite of himself.

Then Joseph went up to the men who were dragging the heavy timbers towards the old house. "I'll give you what your time and labor of bringin' 'em here is worth," he said. As he spoke he drew out his old pocket-book.

The men all stared at him. He became the target of gaping faces, but he did not quail.

"'Ain't you goin' to have the house moved, after all?" asked one man, with a bewildered air.

"No; changed my mind. Goin' to let her set where she is. I'll pay you whatever your time and labor's worth."

After Joseph had paid the men, and had seen the heavy old horse lumber across the field with his burden, he entered his house. There had been a little digging under one of the walls; otherwise it had been untouched. He noticed that, and reflected that he would make it right before sundown. A clump of pinks had been uprooted. He carried them into the house, and put them in a pitcher of water, and they filled the room with their spicy fragrance.  Joseph lived entirely alone, yet the house was very orderly.  He had planned to do most of the housework himself after he was married, and save Sarah.

Joseph sat down awhile in the old rocking-chair beside the sitting-room window, and his heart ached as if it were breaking.  He could scarcely believe in the reality of that which had befallen him; there was in his soul an awful pain of readjustment to its old ways.  But, after all, he had passed his youth and his time of acutest rebellion.  After a while he heard a fluting note of a bird close to the house, and it sounded in his ears like a primal comfort - note of nature.  All at once he was distinctly conscious of a feeling of gladness that the poor old house was not to be torn up by its roots like the

clump of pinks, and set in alien soil.
He had lived in the house so long that at
times it seemed fairly alive to him, and
something which could be hurt. He
looked at the walls lovingly. "Might
have weakened 'em," he said, "and I
always liked this old satin paper."

He looked out of the window, and the
silvery shimmer of the birches and their
white gleam of limb caught his eye. He
got up heavily, put on his old straw hat,
went out of the house, and the solitary
birch which had been bereft of her sisters
was very near. He flung himself down
beside her, and leaned against her frail,
swaying body, and felt her silvery skin
against his cheek, and all at once the
dearness of that which is always left in
the treasure-house of nature for those
who are robbed came over him and
satisfied him. He loved the girl as he

"HE SAT A LONG TIME LEANING AGAINST THE WHITE BIRCH-TREE"

had never loved her before, and his love was so great and unselfish and inno-cent that it overweighed his loss, and it was to him as if he had not lost her at all. With no pain he began to think of her as the bride of the other man.

"He was always a good fellow," he said, "and she ought to marry a man nearer her own age."

He sat a long time leaning against the white birch-tree through whose boughs a soft wind came at intervals, and made a gentle, musical rustle of twinkling leaves, and the tree did not fairly know that the wind was not stirring the leaves of her lost sisters, and the man's love and sense of primeval comfort were so great that he was still filled with the peace of possession.

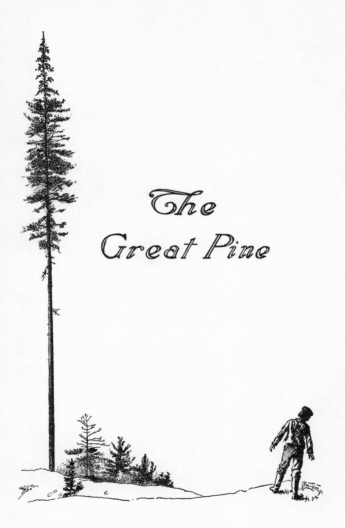

# The Great Pine

# THE GREAT PINE

T was in the summer-time that the great pine sang his loudest song of winter, for always the voice of the tree seemed to arouse in the listener a realization of that which was past and to come, rather than of the present. In the winter the tree seemed to sing of the slumberous peace under his gently fanning boughs, and the deep swell of his aromatic breath in burning noons, and when the summer traveller up the mountain - side threw himself, spent and heated, beneath his shade, then the winter song was at its best. When the wind swelled high came the song of the ice-fields, of the frozen mountain-torrents, of the trees wearing hoary beards and bent double like old men, of the little wild things trembling in their covers when the sharp reports of the frost sounded through the rigid hush of the arctic night and death was abroad. The man who lay beneath the tree had much uncultivated imagination, and, though hampered by exceeding igno-rance, he yet saw and heard that which was beyond mere observation. When exhausted by the summer heat, he re-flected upon the winter with that keen pleasure which comes from the mental grasp of contrast to discomfort. He did not know that he heard the voice of the tree and not his own thought, so did the personality of the great pine

70

"HAD CLIMBED DIFFERENT HEIGHTS FROM MOUNTAINS"

mingle with his own. He was a sailor, and had climbed different heights from mountains, even masts made from the kindred of the tree.

Presently he threw his head back, and stared up and up, and reflected what a fine mast the tree would make, if only it were not soft pine. There was a stir in a branch, and a bird which lived in the tree in summer cast a small, wary glance at him from an eye like a point of bright intelligence, but the man did not see it. He drew a long breath, and looked irresolutely at the upward slope beyond the tree. It was time for him to be up and on if he would cross the mountain before nightfall. He was a wayfarer without resources. He was as poor as the tree, or any of the wild creatures which were in hiding around him on the mountain. He was even poorer, for he had not their feudal tenure of an abiding-place for root and foot on the mountain by the inalienable right of past generations of his race. Even the little, wary - eyed, feathered thing had its small freehold in the branches of the great pine, but the man had nothing. He had returned to primitive conditions; he was portionless save for that with which he came into the world, except for two garments which were nearly past their use as such. His skin showed through the rents; the pockets were empty. Adam expelled from Eden was not in much worse case, and this man also had at his back the flaming sword of punishment for wrong-doing. The man arose. He stood for a moment, letting the cool wind fan his forehead a little longer; then he bent his shoulders

72

doggedly and resumed his climb up the dry bed of a brook which was in winter a fierce conduit for the melting ice and snow. Presently he came to such a choke of fallen trees across the bed that he had to leave it; then there was a sheer rock ascent which he had to skirt and go lower down the mountain to avoid.

The tree was left alone. He stood quiescent with the wind in his green plumes. He belonged to that simplest form of life which cannot project itself beyond its own existence to judge of it. He did not know when presently the man returned and threw himself down with a violent thud against his trunk, though there was a slight shock to his majesty. But the man looked up at the tree and cursed it. He had lost his way through avoiding the rocky precipice, and had circled back to the tree. He remained there a few minutes to gain breath; then he rose, for the western sunlight was filtering in gold drops through the foliage below the pine, and plodded heavily on again.

It might have been twenty minutes before he returned. When he saw the pine he cursed more loudly than before. The sun was quite low. The mountain seemed to be growing in size, the valleys were fast becoming gulfs of black mystery. The man looked at the tree malignantly. He felt in his pocket for a knife which he used to own, then for a match, the accompaniment of the tobacco and pipe which formerly comforted him, but there was none there. The thought of the lost pipe and tobacco filled him with a childish savagery. He felt that he must vent his spite upon something outside himself. He picked up two dry sticks, and began rubbing them together. He had some skill in woodcraft. Presently a spark gleamed; then another. He scraped up a handful of dry leaves. Presently smoke arose pungently in his face, then a flame leaped to life. The man kept on his way, leaving a fire behind him, and swore with an oath that he would not be trapped by the tree again.

He struggled up the old waterway, turning aside for the prostrate skeletons of giant trees, clambering over heaps of stones which might have been the cairns of others, and clawing up precipices like a panther. After one fierce scramble he paused for breath, and, standing on a sheer rock ledge, gazed downward. Below him was a swaying, folding gloom full of vague whispers and rustlings. It seemed to wave and eddy before him like the sea from the deck of a ship, and, indeed, it was another deep, only of air instead of water. Suddenly he realized that there was no light, that the fire which he had kindled must have gone out. He stared into the waving darkness below, and sniffed hard. He could smell smoke faintly, although he could see no fire. Then all at once came a gleam of red, then a leap of orange flame. Then— no human being could have told how it happened, he himself least of all, what swift motive born of deeds and experiences in his own life, born perhaps of deeds and experiences of long-dead ancestors, actuated him. He leaped back down the mountain, stumbling headlong, falling at times, and scrambled to his feet again, sending loose stones down in avalanches, running risks of life and limb, but never faltering until he was beside the pine, standing, singing in the growing glare of the fire. Then he began beating the fire fiercely with sticks, trampling it until he blistered his feet. At last the fire was out. People on a hotel piazza down in the valley, who had been watching it, turned away. "The fire is out," they said, with the regret of those who miss a spectacular delight, although admitting the pity and shame of it, yet coddling with fierce and defiant joy the secret lust of destruction of the whole race. "The fire is out," they said; but more than the fire had burned low, and was out, on the mountain. The man who had evoked destruction to satisfy his own wrath and bitterness of spirit, and then repented, sat for a few minutes outside

the blackened circle around the great
pine, breathing hard. He drew his
rough coat-sleeve across his wet forehead, and stared up at the tree, which
loomed above him like a prophet with
solemnly waving arms of benediction,
prophesying in a great unknown language of his own. He gaped as he
stared; his face looked vacant. He
felt in his pocket for his departed pipe,
then withdrew his hand forcibly, dash-
ing it against the ground. Then he
sighed, swore mildly under his breath
an oath of weariness and misery rather
than of wrath. Then he pulled himself up by successive stages of his stiff
muscles, like an old camel, and resumed
his journey.

After a while he again paused and
looked back. The moon had arisen,
and he could see quite plainly the great

pine standing crowned with white light, tossing his boughs like spears and lances of silver. "Thunderin' big tree," he muttered, with a certain pride and self - approbation. He felt that that majestic thing owed its being to him, to his forbearance with his own hard fate. Had it not been for that it would have been a mere blackened trunk. At that moment, for the first time in his history, he rose superior to his own life. In some unknown fashion this seemingly trivial happening had, as it were, tuned him to a higher place in the scale of things than he had ever held. He, through saving the tree from himself, gained a greater spiritual growth than the tree had gained in height since it first quickened with life. Who shall determine the limit at which the intimate connection and reciprocal influence of all forms of visible creation upon one another may stop? A man may cut down a tree and plant one. Who knows what effect the tree may have upon the man, to his raising or undoing?

Presently the man frowned and shook his head in a curious fashion, as if he questioned his own identity; then he resumed his climb. After the summit was gained he went down the other side of the mountain, then northward through a narrow gorge of valley to which the moonbeams did not yet penetrate. This valley, between mighty walls of silver-crested darkness, was terrifying. The man felt his own smallness and the largeness of nature which seemed about to fall upon him. Spirit was intimidated by matter. The man, rude and unlettered, brutalized and dulled

by his life, yet realized it. He rolled
his eyes aloft from side to side, and ran
as if pursued.

When he had reached the brow of
a little decline in the valley road he
paused and searched eagerly with
straining eyes the side of the mountain
on the right. Then he drew a long
breath of relief. He had seen what
he wished to see—a feeble glimmer of
lamplight from a window of a house,
the only one on that lonely road for five
miles in either direction. It was the
dwelling - house on a small farm which
had been owned by the father of the
woman whom the man had married
fifteen years before. Ten years ago,
when he had run away, there had been
his wife, his little girl, and his wife's
mother living on the farm. The old
farmer father had died two years before

that, and the man, who had wild blood
in his veins, had rebelled at the hard
grind necessary to wrest a livelihood
by himself from the mountain soil. So
one morning he was gone, leaving a
note saying that he had gone to sea,
and would write and send money, that
he could earn more than on a farm.
But he never wrote, and he never sent
the money. He had met with sin and
disaster, and at last he started homeward, shorn, and, if not repentant, weary
of wrong-doing and its hard wages. He
had retreated from the broad way with
an ignoble impulse, desiring the safety
of the narrow, and the loaves and
fishes, which, after all, can be found in
it with greater certainty; but now, as
he hastened along, he became conscious
of something better than that. One
good impulse begat others by some law

of spiritual reproduction. He began to think how he would perhaps do more work than he had formerly, and please his wife and her mother.

He looked at the light in the window ahead with something akin to thankfulness. He remembered how very gentle his wife had been, and how fond of him. His wife's mother also had been a mild woman, with reproving eyes only, never with a tongue of reproach. He remembered his little girl with a thrill of tenderness and curiosity. She would be a big girl now; she would be like her mother. He began picturing to himself what they would do and say, what they would give him for supper. He thought he would like a slice of ham cut from one of those cured on the farm, that and some new-laid eggs. He would have some of those biscuits that his wife's mother used to make, and some fresh butter, and honey from the home bees. He would have tea and cream. He seemed to smell the tea and the ham. A hunger which was sorer than any hunger of the flesh came over him. All at once the wanderer starved for home. He had been ship-wrecked and at the point of death from hunger, but never was hunger like this. He had planned speeches of con-trition; now he planned nothing. He feared no blame from those whom he had wronged; he feared nothing ex-cept his own need of them. Faster and faster he went. He seemed to be run-ning a race. At last he was quite close to the house. The light was in a win-dow facing the road, and the curtain was up. He could see a figure steadily passing and repassing it. He went

closer, and saw that it was a little girl
with a baby in her arms, and she was
walking up and down hushing it. A
feeble cry smote his ears, though the
doors and windows were closed. It was
chilly even in midsummer in the mountains. He went around the house to the
side door. He noticed that the field
on the left was waving with tall, dry
grass, which should have been cut long
ago; he noticed that there were no bean-
poles in the garden. He noticed that
the house looked gray and shabby even
in the moonlight, that some blinds were
gone and a window broken. He leaned
a second against the door. Then he
opened it and entered. He came into
a little, square entry; on one side was
the kitchen door, on the other the room
where the light was. He opened the
door leading to this room. He stood

staring, for nothing which he had antici-
pated met his eyes, except the little girl.
She stood gazing at him, half in alarm,
half in surprise, clutching close the
baby, which was puny, but evidently
about a year old.   Two little boys stood
near the table on which the lamp was
burning, and they stared at him with
wide - open mouths and round eyes.
But the sight which filled the intruder
with the most amazement and dismay
was that of a man in the bed in the
corner.   He recognized him at once as
a farmer who had lived, at the time of
his departure, five miles away in the
village.   He remembered that his wife
was recently dead when he left.   The
man, whose blue, ghastly face was
sunken in the pillows, looked up at him.
He thrust out a cadaverous hand as if
to threaten.   The little girl with the

baby and the two little boys edged
nearer the bed, as if for protection.

"Who be you?" inquired the sick
man, with feeble menace. "What d' ye
want comin' in here this way?" It was
like the growl of a sick dog.

The other man went close to the bed.
"Where is my wife?" he asked, in a
strange voice. It was expressive of
horror and anger and a rage of disappointment.

"You ain't—Dick?" gasped the man
in bed.

"Yes, I be; and I know you, Johnny
Willet. Where is my wife? What are
you here for?"

"Your wife is dead," answered the
man, in a choking voice. He began to
cough; he half raised himself on one
elbow. His eyes bulged. He crowed
like a child with the croup. The little

girl promptly laid the baby on the bed
and ran to a chimney cupboard for a
bottle of medicine, which she adminis-
tered with a spoon. The sick man lay
back, gasping for breath. He looked
as if already dead; his jaw dropped;
there were awful blue hollows in his
face.

"Dead!" repeated the visitor, thinking of his wife, and not of the other
image of death before him.

"Yes, she's dead."

"Where's my little girl?"

The sick man raised one shaking
hand and pointed to the little girl who
had taken up the whimpering baby.

"That?"

The sick man nodded.

The other eyed the little girl, rather
tall for her age, but very slim, her narrow shoulders already bent with toil.

She regarded him, with serious blue eyes in a little face, with an expression of gentleness so pronounced that it gave the impression of a smile. The man's eyes wandered from the girl to the baby in her arms and the two little boys.

"What be you all a-doin' here?" he demanded, gruffly, and made a movement towards the bed. The little girl turned pale, and clutched the baby more closely. The sick man made a feeble sound of protest and deprecation. "What be you all a-doin' here?" demanded the other again.

"I married your wife after we heard your ship was lost. We knew you was aboard her from Abel Dennison. He come home, and said you was dead for sure, some eight year ago, and then she said she'd marry me. I'd been after her some time. My wife died, and my house burned down, and I was left alone without any home, and I'd always liked her. She wasn't any too willin', but finally she give in."

The man whom he had called Dick glared at him speechlessly.

"We both thought you was dead, sure," said the sick man, in a voice of mild deprecation, which was ludicrously out of proportion to the subject.

Dick looked at the children.

"We had 'em," said the sick man. "She died when the baby was two months old, and your girl Lottie has been taking care of it. It has been pretty hard for her, but I was took sick, and 'ain't been able to do anything. I can jest crawl round a little, and that's all. Lottie can milk—we've got one cow left—and she feeds the hens, and my first wife's brother has given us some flour and meal, and cuts up some wood to burn, and we've worried along, but we can't stand it when winter comes, anyhow. Somethin' has got to be done." Suddenly an expression of blank surprise before an acquisition of knowledge came over his face. "Good Lord! Dick," he gasped out, "it's all yours. It's all yours, anyway, now."

"Where's the old woman?" asked Dick, abruptly, ignoring what the other said.

"Your wife's mother? She died of pneumonia about two year ago. Your wife she took it to heart pretty bad. She was a heap of help about the children."

Dick nodded. "The old woman always was smart to work," he assented.

"Yes, and your wife she wa'n't over-strong."

"Never was."

"No."

"S'pose there was enough to put her away decent?"

"I sold the wood-lot on the back road. There's a gravestone. Luckily I had it done before I was took sick."

"S'pose you're pretty hard pinched now?"

"Awful hard. We can't get along so much longer. There's enough wood to cut, if I could do it, that would bring in somethin'; and there's the hay, that's spoilin'. I can't do nothin'. There's nothin' but this house over our heads." Suddenly that look of surprised knowledge came over his face again. "Lord! it's all yours, and the girl's, anyhow," he muttered.

"She's been doin' the work?" asked Dick, pointing to the girl.

"Yes; she does the best she can, but she ain't very big, and the children 'ain't got enough to be decent, and we can't get much cooked."

Dick made a resolute step towards the door.

"Where be you a-goin', Dick?" asked the sick man, with a curious wistfulness. "You ain't goin' to-night?"

"What is there in the house to eat?"

"What's in the house, Lottie?"

"There's some meal and milk and eggs," answered the child, in a high, sweet voice.

"Come here and give us a kiss, Lottie," said Dick, suddenly.

The little girl approached him timidly, staggering under the weight of the baby. She lifted her face, and the man kissed her with a sort of solemnity. "I'm your father, Lottie," said he.

The two looked at each other, the child shrinking, yet smiling.

"Glad I got home?" asked the man.

"Yes, sir."

Dick went out into the kitchen, and the children followed and stood in the doorway, watching. He gravely set to work with such utensils and materials as he found, which were scanty enough. He kindled a fire and made a corn-cake. He made porridge for the sick man and carried him a bowl of it smoking hot. "'Ain't had nothin' like this sence she died," said the sick man.

After supper Dick cleaned the kitchen. He also tidied up the other room and made the bed, and milked, and split some wood wherewith to cook breakfast.

"You ain't goin' to - night, Dick?" the sick man said, anxiously, when he came in after the work was done.

"No, I ain't."

"Lord! I forgot; it's your house," said the sick man.

"I wa'n't goin' anyhow," said Dick.

"Well, there's a bed up-stairs. You 'ain't got any more clothes than what you've got on, have you?"

"No, I 'ain't," replied Dick, shortly.

"Well, there's mine in the closet out of this room, and you might jest as well wear 'em till I get up. There's some shirts and some pants."

"All right," said Dick.

The next morning Dick got the breakfast, cooking eggs with wonderful skill and frying corn - cakes. Then, dressed in the sick man's shirt and trousers, he set forth, axe in hand. He

toiled all day in the woods; he toiled
every day until he had sufficient wood
cut, then he hired a horse, to be paid
for when the wood was sold.   He carted
loads to the hotels and farm - houses
where summer - boarders were taken.
He arose before dawn and worked in the
field and garden.   He cut the hay.   He
was up half the night setting the house
to rights.   He washed and ironed like
a woman.   The whole establishment
was transformed.   He got a doctor for
the sick man, but he gave small en-
couragement.   He had consumption,
although he might linger long.   "Who's
going to take care of the poor fellow, I don't know," said the doctor.

"I be," said Dick.

"Then there are the children," said
the doctor.

"GET UP!" HE CRIED, HARSHLY

"One of 'em is mine, and I'll take care of his," said Dick.

The doctor stared, as one stares who sees a good deed in a naughty world, with a mixture of awe, of contempt, and of incredulity.

"Well," he said, "it's lucky you came along."

After that Dick simply continued in his new path of life. He worked and nursed. It was inconceivable how much the man accomplished. He developed an enormous capacity for work. In the autumn he painted the house; the cellar was full of winter vegetables, the wood-pile was compact. The children were warmly clad, and Lottie went to school. Her father had bought an old horse for a song, and he carried her to school every day. Once in January he had occasion to drive around the

SIX TREES

other side of the mountain which he
had climbed the night of his return.
He started early in the afternoon, that
he might be in season to go for Lottie.

It was a clear, cold day. Snow was
on the ground, a deep, glittering level,
with a hard crust of ice. The sleigh slid
over the frozen surface with long hiss-
es. The trees were all bare and had
suffered frightfully in the last storm.
The rain had frozen as it fell, and there
had been a high gale. The ice-mailed
branches had snapped, and sometimes
whole trees. Dick, slipping along on
the white line of road below, gazed up
at the side of the mountain. He looked
and looked again. Then he desisted.
He reached over and cut the horse's
back with the reins. "Get up!" he
cried, harshly.

The great pine had fallen from his

high estate.   He was no more to be seen dominating the other trees, standing out in solitary majesty among his kind.   The storm had killed him.   He lay prostrate on the mountain.

And the man on the road below passed like the wind, and left the mountain and the dead tree behind.

# The Balsam Fir

# THE BALSAM FIR

MARTHA ELDER had lived alone for years on Amesboro road, a mile from the nearest neighbor, three miles from the village. She lived in the low cottage which her grandfather had built. It was painted white, and there was a green trellis over the front door shaded by a beautiful rose-vine. Martha had very little money, but somehow she always managed to keep her house in good order, though she had never had any blinds. It had always been the dream of Martha's life to have blinds;

her mild blue eyes were very sensitive to the glare of strong sunlight, and the house faced west. Sometimes of a summer afternoon Martha waxed fairly rebellious because of her lack of green blinds to soften the ardent glare. She had green curtains, but they flapped in the wind and made her nervous, and she could not have them drawn.

Blinds were not the only things which aroused in Martha Elder a no less strong, though unexpressed, spirit of rebellion against the smallness of her dole of the good things of life. Nobody had ever heard this tall, fair, gentle woman utter one word of complaint. She spoke and moved with mild grace. The sweetest acquiescence seemed evident in her every attitude of body and tone of voice. People said that Martha Elder was an old maid, that she was all alone in the world, that she had a hard time to get along and keep out of the poor-house, but that she was perfectly contented and happy. But people did not know; she had her closets of passionate solitude to which they did not penetrate. When her sister Adeline, ten years after her father's death, had married the man who everybody had thought would marry Martha, she had made a pretty wedding for her, and people had said Martha did not care, after all; that she was cut out for an old maid; that she did not want to marry. Nobody knew, not her sister, not even the man himself, who had really given her reason to blame him, how she felt. She was encased in an armor of womanly pride as impenetrable as a coat of mail; it was proof against everything except the arrows of agony of her own secret longings.

Martha had been a very pretty girl, much prettier than her younger sister Adeline; it was strange that she had not been preferred; it was strange that she had not had suitors in plenty; but there may have been something about the very fineness of her femininity and its perfection which made it repellent. Adeline, with her coarse bloom and loud laugh and ready stare, had always had admirers by the score, while Martha, who was really exquisite, used to go to bed and lie awake listening to the murmur of voices under the green trellis of the front door, until the man who married her sister came. Then for a brief space his affections did verge towards Martha; he said various things to her in a voice whose cadences ever after made her music of life; he looked at her with an expression which became photographed, as by some law of love instead of light, on her heart. Then Adeline, exuberant with passion, incredulous that he could turn to her sister instead of herself, won him away by her strong pull upon the earthy part of him. Martha had not dreamed of contesting the matter, of making a fight for the man whom she loved. She yielded at once with her pride so exquisite that it seemed like meekness.

When Adeline went away, she settled down at once into her solitary old-maiden estate, although she was still comparatively young. She had her little ancestral house, her small vegetable garden, a tiny wood-lot from which she hired enough wood cut to supply her needs, and a very small sum of money in the bank, enough to pay her taxes and insurance, and not much

besides. She had a few hens, and lived
mostly on eggs and vegetables; as for
her clothes, she never wore them out;
she moved about softly and carefully,
and never frayed the hems of her gowns,
nor rubbed her elbows; and as for soil,
no mortal had ever seen a speck of
grime upon Martha Elder or her rai-
ment. She seemed to pick her spotless
way through life like a white dove.
There was a story that Martha once
wore a white dress all one summer,
keeping it immaculate without washing,
and it seemed quite possible. When
she walked abroad she held her dress
skirt at an unvarying height of modest
neatness revealing snowy starched pet-
ticoats and delicate ankles in white
stockings. She might have been painted as a type of elderly maiden peace
and pure serenity by an artist who

could see only externals. But it was very different with her from what people thought. Nobody dreamed of the fierce tension of her nerves as she sat at her window sewing through the long summer afternoons, drawing her monotonous thread in and out of dainty seams; nobody dreamed what revolt that little cottage roof, when it was covered with wintry snows, sometimes sheltered. When Martha's sister came home with her husband and beautiful first baby to visit her, her smiling calm of welcome was inimitable.

"Martha never did say much," Adeline told her husband, when they were in their room at night. "She didn't exclaim even over the baby." As she spoke she looked gloatingly at his rosy curves as he lay asleep. "Martha's an old maid if there ever was one," she added.

"It's queer, for she's pretty," said her husband.

"I don't call her pretty," said Adeline; "not a mite of color." She glanced at her high bloom and tossing black mane of hair in the mirror.

"Yes, that's so," agreed Adeline's husband. Still, sometimes he used to look at Martha with the old expression, unconsciously, even before his wife, but Martha never recognized it for the same. When he had married her sister he had established between himself and her such a veil of principle that her eyes never after could catch the true meaning of him. Yet nobody knew how glad she was when this little family outside her pale of life had gone, and she could settle back unmolested

"'SHE DIDN'T EXCLAIM EVEN OVER THE BABY'"

into her own tracks, which were apparently those of peace, but in reality those of a caged panther. There was a strip of carpet worn threadbare in the sitting-room by Martha's pacing up and down. At last she had to take out that breadth and place it next the wall, and replace it.

People wondered why, with all Martha's sweetness and serenity, she had not professed religion and united with the church. When the minister came to talk with her about it he was nonplussed. She said, with an innocent readiness which abashed him, that she believed in the Christian religion, and trusted that she loved God; then it was as if she folded wings of concealment over her maiden character, and he could see no more.

It was at last another woman to

whom she unbosomed herself, and she was a safe confidante; no safer could have been chosen. She was a far-removed cousin, and stone - deaf from scarlet fever when she was a baby. She was a woman older than Martha, and had come to make her a visit. She lived with a married sister, to whom she was a burden, and who was glad to be rid of her for a few weeks. She could not hear one word that was spoken to her; she could only distinguish language uncertainly from the motion of the lips. She was absolutely penniless, except for a little which she earned by knitting cotton lace. To this woman Martha laid bare her soul the day before Christmas, as the two sat by the western windows, one knitting, the other darning a pair of white stockings.

"To-morrow's Christmas," said the

deaf woman, suddenly, in her strange, unmodulated voice. She had a flat, pale face, with smooth loops of blond hair around the temples.

Martha said, "It ain't much Christmas to me."

"What?" returned the deaf woman.

"It ain't much Christmas to me," repeated Martha. She did not raise her voice in the least, and she moved her lips very little. Speech never disturbed the sweet serenity of her mouth. The deaf woman did not catch a word, but she was always sensitive about asking over for the second time. She knitted and acted as if she understood.

"No, it ain't much Christmas to me, and it never has been," said Martha. "I 'ain't never felt as if I had had any Christmas, for my part. I don't know where it has come in if I have. I never had a Christmas present in my whole life, unless I count in that purple crocheted shawl that Adeline gave me, that somebody gave her, and she couldn't wear, because it wasn't becomin'. I never thought much of it myself. Purple never suited me, either. That was the only Christmas present I ever had. That came a week after Christmas, ten year ago, and I suppose I might count that in. I kept it laid away, and the moths got into it."

"What?" said the deaf woman.

"The moths got into it," said Martha. The deaf woman nodded wisely and knitted.

"Christmas!" said Martha, with a scorn at once pathetic and bitter—"talk about Christmas! What is Christmas to a woman all alone in the

world as I am? If you want to see the
loneliest thing in all creation, look at
a woman all alone in the world. Adeline is twenty - five miles away, and
she's got her family. I'm all alone. I
might as well be at the north pole.
What's Christmas to a woman without
children, or any other women to think
about, livin' with her? If I had any
money to give it might be different. I
might find folks to give to — other
folks's children; but I'ain't got any money. I've got nothing. I can't give any
Christmas presents myself, and I can't
have any. Lord! Talk about Christmas to me! I can't help if I am wicked.
I'm sick and tired of livin'. I have
been for some time." Just then a farmer's team loaded with evergreens surmounted with merry boys went by, and
she pointed tragically; and the deaf

woman's eyes followed her pointing finger, and suddenly her great, smiling face changed. "There they go with Christmas - trees for other women," said Martha; "for women who have got what I haven't. I never had a Christmas-tree. I never had a Christmas. The Lord never gave me one. I want one Christmas before I die. I've got a right to it. I want one Christmas-tree and one Christmas." Her voice rose to daring impetus; the deaf woman looked at her curiously.

"What?" said she.

"I want one Christmas," said Martha. Still the deaf woman did not hear, but suddenly the calm of her face broke up; she began to weep. It was as if she understood the other's mood by some subtler faculty than that of hearing. "Christmas is a pretty sad day to me,"

116

said she, "ever since poor mother died.
I always realize more than any other
time how alone I be, and how my room
would be better than my company,
and I don't ever have any presents.
And I can't give any. I give all my
knittin' money to Jane for my board,
and that ain't near enough. Oh, Lord!
it's a hard world!"

"I want one Christmas, and one
Christmas-tree," said Martha, in a singu-
lar tone, almost as if she were demand-
ing it of some unseen power.

"What?" said the deaf woman.

"I want one Christmas, and one
Christmas-tree," repeated Martha.

The deaf woman nodded and knitted, after wiping her eyes. Her face
was still quivering with repressed emo-
tion.

Martha rose. "Well, there's no use

talkin'," said she, in a hard voice; "folks can take what they get in this world, not what they want, I s'pose." Her face softened a little as she looked at the deaf woman. "I guess I'll make some toast for supper; there's enough milk," said she.

"What?" said the deaf woman.

Martha put her lips close to her ear, and shouted, "I guess I'll make some toast for supper." The deaf woman caught the word toast, and smiled happily, with a sniff of retreating grief; she was very fond of toast. "Jane 'most never has it," said she. As she sat there beside the window, she presently smelled the odor of toast coming in from the kitchen; then it began to snow. The snow fell in great, damp blobs, coating all the trees thickly. When Martha entered the sitting-room to get a dish from the china-closet the deaf woman pointed, and said it was snowing.

"Yes, I see it is," replied Martha. "Well, it can snow, for all me. I 'ain't got any Christmas-tree to go to to-night."

As she spoke, both she and the deaf woman, looking out of the window, noted the splendid fir-balsam opposite, and at the same time a man with an axe, preparing to cut it down.

"Why, that man's goin' to cut down that tree! Ain't it on your land?" cried the deaf woman.

Martha shrieked and ran out of the house, bareheaded in the dense fall of snow. She caught hold of the man's arm, and he turned and looked at her with a sort of stolid surprise fast strengthening into obstinacy. "What you cuttin' down this tree for?" asked Martha.

The man muttered that he had been sent for one for Lawyer Ede.

"Well, you can't have mine," said Martha. "This ain't Lawyer Ede's land. His is on the other side of the fence. There are trees plenty good enough over there. You let mine be."

The man's arm which held the axe twitched. Suddenly Martha snatched it away by such an unexpected motion that he yielded. Then she was mistress of the situation. She stood before the tree, brandishing the axe. "If you dare to come one step nearer my tree, I'll kill you," said she. The man paled. He was a stolid farmer, unused to women like her, or, rather, unused to such developments in wom-

"'THERE ARE TREES PLENTY GOOD ENOUGH OVER THERE'"

en like her. "Give me that axe," he
said.

"I'll give you that axe if you promise to cut down one of Lawyer Ede's
trees, and let mine be!"

"All right," assented the man, sulkily.

"You go over the wall, then, and I'll
hand you the axe."

The man, with a shuffling of reluctant yielding, approached the wall and
climbed over. Then Martha yielded up
the axe. Then she stationed herself in
front of her tree, to make sure that it
was not harmed. The snow fell thick
and fast on her uncovered head, but she
did not mind. She remembered how
once the man who had married her
sister had said something to her beside
this tree, when it was young like herself. She remembered long summer
afternoons of her youth looking out

upon it. Her old dreams and hopes of youth seemed still abiding beneath it, greeting her like old friends. She felt that she would have been killed herself rather than have the tree harmed. The soothing fragrance of it came in her face. She felt suddenly as if the tree were alive. A great, protecting tenderness for it came over her. She began to hear axe strokes on the other side of the wall. Then the deaf woman came to the door of the house, and stood there staring at her through the damp veil of snow. "You'll get your death out there, Marthy," she called out.

"No, I won't," replied Martha, knowing as she spoke that she was not heard.

"What be you stayin' out there for?" called the deaf woman, in an alarmed voice. Martha made no reply.

Presently the woman came out through the snow; she paused before she reached her; it was quite evident what she feared even before she spoke. "Be you crazy?" asked she.

"I'm going to see to it that John Page don't cut down this tree," replied Martha. "I know how set the Pages are." The deaf woman stared helplessly at her, not hearing a word.

Then John Page came to the wall. "Look at here," he called out. "I ain't goin' to tech your tree. I thought it was on Ede's land. I'm cuttin' down another."

"You mind you don't," responded Martha, and she hardly knew her voice. When John Page went home that night he told his wife that he'd "never known that Martha Elder was such an up and comin' woman. Deliver me from dealin' with old maids," said he; "they're worse than barbed wire."

The snow continued until midnight, then the rain set in, then it cleared and froze. When the sun rose next morning everything was coated with ice. The fir-balsam was transfigured, wonderful. Every little twig glittered as with the glitter of precious stones, the branches spread low in rainbow radiances. Martha and the deaf woman stood at the sitting-room window looking out at it. Martha's face changed as she looked. She put her face close to the other woman's ear and shouted: "Look here, Abby, you ain't any too happy with Jane; you stay here with me this winter. I'm lonesome, and we'll get along somehow." The deaf woman heard her, and

"STOOD STARING AT THE GLORIFIED FIR-BALSAM"

a great light came into her flat countenance.

"Stay with you?"

Martha nodded.

"I earn enough to pay for the flour and sugar," said she, eagerly, "and you've got vegetables in the cellar, and I don't want another thing to eat, and I'll do all the work if you'll let me, Marthy."

"I'll be glad to have you stay," said Martha, with the eagerness of one who grasps at a treasure.

"Do you mean you want me to stay?" asked the deaf woman, wistfully, still fearing that she had not heard aright. Martha nodded.

"I'll go out in the kitchen and make some of them biscuit I used to make for breakfast," said the deaf woman. "God bless you, Marthy!"

Martha stood staring at the glorified fir-balsam. All at once it seemed to her that she saw herself, as she was in her youth, under it. Old possessions filled her soul with rapture, and the conviction of her inalienable birthright of the happiness of life was upon her. She also seemed to see all the joys which she had possessed or longed for in the radius of its radiance; its boughs seemed overladen with fulfilment and promise, and a truth came to her for the great Christmas present of her life. She became sure that whatever happiness God gives He never retakes, and, moreover, that He holds ready the food for all longing, that one cannot exist without the other.

"Whatever I've ever had that I loved I've got," said Martha Elder, "and whatever I've wanted I'm goin' to have." Then she turned around and went out in the kitchen to help about breakfast, and the dazzle of the Christmas-tree was so great in her eyes that she was almost blinded to all the sordid conditions of her daily life.

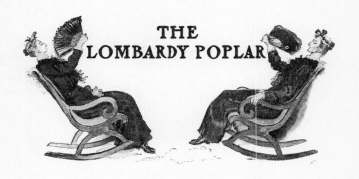

# THE
# LOMBARDY POPLAR

# THE LOMBARDY POPLAR

**T**HERE had been five in the family of the Lombardy poplar. Formerly he had stood before the Dunn house in a lusty row of three brothers and a mighty father, from whose strong roots, extending far under the soil, they had all sprung.

Now they were all gone, except this one, the last of the sons of the tree. He alone remained, faithful as a sentinel before the onslaught of winter storms and summer suns; he yielded to neither. He was head and shoulders above the

other trees — the cherry and horse-
chestnuts in the square front yard behind him. Higher than the house,
piercing the blue with his broad trun-
cate of green, he stood silent, stiff,
and immovable. He seldom made any
sound with his closely massed foliage,
and it required a mighty and concentrated gust of wind to sway him ever so
little from his straight perpendicular.

As the tree was the last of his imme-
diate family, so the woman who lived
in the house was the last of hers. Sarah
Dunn was the only survivor of a large
family. No fewer than nine children had
been born to her parents; now father,
mother, and eight children were all dead,
and this elderly woman was left alone in
the old house. Consumption had been
in the Dunn family. The last who had
succumbed to it was Sarah's twin-sis-

ter Marah, and she had lived until both had gray hair.

After that last funeral, where she was the solitary real mourner, there being only distant relatives of the Dunn name, Sarah closed all the house except a few rooms, and resigned herself to living out her colorless life alone. She seldom went into any other house; she had few visitors, with the exception of one woman. She was a second cousin, of the same name, being also Sarah Dunn. She came regularly on Thursday afternoons, stayed to tea, and went to the evening prayer - meeting. Besides the sameness of name, there was a remarkable resemblance in personal appearance between the two women. They were of about the same age; they both had gray - blond hair, which was very thin, and strained painfully back from

133

their ears and necks into tiny rosettes
at the backs of their heads, below little,
black lace caps trimmed with bows of
purple ribbon.  The cousin Sarah had
not worn the black lace cap until the
other Sarah's twin-sister Marah had
died.  Then all the dead woman's ward-
robe had been given to her, since she was
needy.  Sarah and her twin had always
dressed alike, and there were many in
the village who never until the day of
her death had been able to distinguish
Marah from Sarah.  They were alike
not only in appearance, but in character.
The resemblance was so absolute as to
produce a feeling of something at fault
in the beholder.  It was difficult, when
looking from one to the other, to believe that the second was a vital fact; it
was like seeing double.  After Marah
was dead it was the same with the

cousin, Sarah Dunn. The clothes of the deceased twin completed all that had been necessary to make the resemblance perfect. There was in the whole Dunn family a curious endurance of characteristics. It was said in the village that you could tell a Dunn if you met him at the ends of the earth. They were all described as little, and sloping-shouldered, and peak-chinned, and sharp-nosed, and light-livered. Sarah and Cousin Sarah were all these. The family tricks of color and form and feature were represented to their fullest extent in both. People said that they were Dunns from the soles of their feet to the crowns of their heads. They did not even use plurals in dealing with them. When they set out together for evening meeting in the summer twilight, both moving with the same gentle, minc-

ing step, the same slight sway of
shoulders, draped precisely alike with
little, knitted, white wool shawls, the
same deprecating cant of heads, identi-
cally bonneted, as if they were per-
petually avoiding some low-hanging
bough of life in their way of progress,
the neighbors said, "There's Sarah Dunn
goin' to meetin'."

When the twin was alive it was,
"There's Sarah and Marah goin' to
meetin'." Even the very similar names
had served as a slight distinction, as
formerly the different dress of the cous-
ins had made it easier to distinguish
between them. Now there was no
difference between the outward characteristics of the two Sarah Dunns, even
to a close observer. Name, appearance, dress, all were identical. And the
minds of the two seemed to partake of

this similarity. Their conversation consisted mainly of a peaceful monotony of agreement. "For the Lord's sake, Sarah Dunn, 'ain't you got any mind of your own?" cried a neighbor of an energetic and independent turn, once when she had run in of a Thursday afternoon when the cousin was there. Sarah looked at the cousin before replying, and the two minds seemed to cogitate the problem through the medium of mild, pale eyes, set alike under faint levels of eyebrow. "For the Lord's sake, if you ain't lookin' at each other to find out!" cried the neighbor, with a high sniff, while the two other women stared at each other in a vain effort to understand.

The twin had been dead five years, and the cousin had come every Thursday afternoon to see Sarah before any

point of difference in their mental atti-
tudes was evident.  They regarded the
weather with identical emotions, they
relished the same food, they felt the
same degree of heat or cold, they had
the same likes and dislikes for other
people, but at last there came a dis-
agreement.  It was on a Thursday in
summer, when the heat was intense.
The cousin had come along the dusty
road between the white-powdered weeds
and flowers, holding above her head
an umbrella small and ancient, covered
with faded green silk, which had belonged to Marah, wearing an old purple
muslin of the dead woman's, and her
black lace mitts.  Sarah was at home,
rocking in the south parlor window,
dressed in the mate to the purple
muslin, fanning herself with a small
black fan edged with feathers which

gave out a curious odor of mouldy roses.

When the cousin entered, she laid aside her bonnet and mitts, and seated herself opposite Sarah, and fanned herself with the mate to the fan.

"It is dreadful warm," said the cousin.

"Dreadful!" said Sarah.

"Seems to me it 'ain't been so warm since that hot Sabbath the summer after Marah died," said the cousin, with gentle reminiscence.

"Just what I was thinking," said Sarah.

"An' it's dusty, too, just as it was then."

"Yes, it was dreadful dusty then. I got my black silk so full of dust it was just about ruined, goin' to meetin' that Sabbath," said Sarah.

"An' I was dreadful afraid I had sp'ilt Marah's, an' she always kept it so nice."

"Yes, she had always kept it dreadful nice," assented Sarah.

"Yes, she had. I 'most wished, when I got home that afternoon, and saw how dusty it was, that she'd kept it and been laid away in it, instead of my havin' it, but I knew she'd said to wear it, and get the good of it, and never mind."

"Yes, she would."

"And I got the dust all off it with a piece of her old black velvet bunnit," said the cousin, with mild deprecation.

"That's the way I got the dust off mine, with a piece of my old black velvet bunnit," said Sarah.

"It's better than anything else to take the dust off black silk."

"Yes, 'tis."

"I saw Mis' Andrew Dunn as I was comin' past," said the cousin.

"I saw her this mornin' down to the store," said Sarah.

"I thought she looked kind of pin-dlin', and she coughed some."

"She did when I saw her. I thought she looked real miserable. Shouldn't wonder if she was goin in the same way as the others."

"Just what I think."

"It was funny we didn't get the consumption, ain't it, when all our folks died with it?"

"Yes, it is funny."

"I s'pose we wa'n't the kind to."

"Yes, I s'pose so."

Then the two women swayed peacefully back and forth in their rocking-chairs, and fluttered their fans gently before their calm faces.

"It is too hot to sew to-day," re-marked Sarah Dunn.

"Yes, it is," assented her cousin.

"I thought I wouldn't bake biscuit for supper, long as it was so dreadful hot."

"I was hopin' you wouldn't. It's too hot for hot biscuit. They kind of go against you."

"That's what I said. Says I, now I ain't goin' to heat up the house bakin' hot bread to-night. I know she won't want me to."

"No, you was just right. I don't."

"Says I, I've got some good cold bread and butter, and blackberries that I bought of the little Whitcomb boy this mornin', and a nice custard - pie, and two kinds of cake besides cookies, and I guess that 'll do."

"That's just what I should have pick-ed out for supper."

"And I thought we'd have it early, so as to get it cleared away, and take our time walkin' to meetin', it's so dreadful hot."

"Yes, it's a good idea."

"I s'pose there won't be so many to meetin', it's so hot," said Sarah.

"Yes, I s'pose so."

"It's queer folks can stay away from meetin' on account of the weather."

"It don't mean much to them that do," said the cousin, with pious rancor.

"That's so," said Sarah. "I guess it don't. I guess it ain't the comfort to them that it is to me. I guess if some of them had lost as many folks as I have they'd go whether 'twas hot or cold."

"I guess they would. They don't know much about it."

Sarah gazed sadly and reflectively

out of the window at the deep yard, with its front gravel walk bordered with wilting pinks and sprawling peonies, its horse-chestnut and cherry trees, and its solitary Lombardy poplar set in advance, straight and stiff as a sentinel of summer. "Speakin' of losin' folks," she said, "you 'ain't any idea what a blessin' that popple-tree out there has been to me, especially since Marah died."

Then, for the first time, the cousin stopped waving her fan in unison, and the shadow of a different opinion darkened her face. "That popple-tree?" she said, with harsh inquiry.

"Yes, that popple-tree." Sarah continued gazing at the tree, standing in majestic isolation, with its long streak of shadow athwart the grass.

The cousin looked, too; then she

turned towards Sarah with a frown of puzzled dissent verging on irritability and scorn. "That popple-tree! Land! how you do talk!" said she. "What sort of a blessin' can an old tree be when your folks are gone, Sarah Dunn?"

Sarah faced her with stout affirmation: "I've seen that popple there ever since I can remember, and it's all I've got left that's anyways alive, and it seems like my own folks, and I can't help it."

The cousin sniffed audibly. She resumed fanning herself, with violent jerks. "Well," said she, "if you can feel as if an old popple-tree made up to you, in any fashion, for the loss of your own folks, and if you can feel as if it was them, all I've got to say is, I can't."

"I'm thankful I can," said Sarah Dunn.

"Well, I can't. It seems to me as if it was almost sacrilegious."

"I can't help how it seems to you." There was a flush of nervous indignation on Sarah Dunn's pale, flaccid cheeks; her voice rang sharp. The resemblance between the two faces, which had in reality been more marked in expression, as evincing a perfect accord of mental action, than in feature even, had almost disappeared.

"An old popple-tree!" said the cousin, with a fury of sarcasm. "If it had been any other tree than a popple, it wouldn't strike anybody as quite so bad. I've always thought a popple was about the homeliest tree that grows. Much as ever as it does grow. It just stays, stiff and pointed, as if it was goin' to make a hole in the sky; don't give no shade worth anything; don't seem to have

146

much to do with the earth and folks, anyhow. I was thankful when I got mine cut down. Them three that was in front of our house were always an eyesore to me, and I talked till I got father to cut them down. I always wondered why you hung on to this one so."

"I wouldn't have that popple-tree cut down for a hundred dollars," declared Sarah Dunn. She had closed her fan, and she held it up straight like a weapon.

"My land! Well, if I was goin' to make such a fuss over a tree I'd have taken something different from a popple. I'd have taken a pretty elm or a maple. They look something like trees. This don't look like anything on earth besides itself. It ain't a tree. It's a stick tryin' to look like one."

"That's why I like it," replied Sarah
Dunn, with a high lift of her head. She
gave a look of sharp resentment at her
cousin. Then she gazed at the tree
again, and her whole face changed in-
describably. She seemed like another
person. The tree seemed to cast a
shadow of likeness over her. She appeared straighter, taller; all her lines of
meek yielding, or scarcely even anything so strong as yielding, of utter
passiveness, vanished. She looked stiff
and uncompromising. Her mouth was
firm, her chin high, her eyes steady, and,
more than all, there was over her an
expression of individuality which had
not been there before. "That's why
I like the popple," said she, in an in-
cisive voice. "That's just why. I'm
sick of things and folks that are just
like everything and everybody else.

I'm sick of trees that are just trees. I like one that ain't."

"My land!" ejaculated the cousin, in a tone of contempt not unmixed with timidity. She stared at the other woman with shrinking and aversion in her pale-blue eyes. "What has come over you, Sarah Dunn?" said she, at last, with a feeble attempt to assert herself.

"Nothin' has come over me. I always felt that way about that popple."

"Marah wa'n't such a fool about that old popple."

"No, she wa'n't, but maybe she would have been if I had been taken first instead of her. Everybody has got to have something to lean on."

"Well, I 'ain't got anything any more than you have, but I can stand up straight without an old popple."

"You 'ain't no call to talk that way," said Sarah.

"I hate to hear folks that I've always thought had common - sense talk like fools," said the cousin, with growing courage.

"If you don't like to hear me talk, it's always easy enough to get out of hearin' distance."

"I'd like to know what you mean by that, Sarah Dunn."

"I mean it just as you want to take it."

"Maybe you mean that my room is better than my company."

"Just as you are a mind to take it."

The cousin sat indeterminately for a few minutes. She thought of the bread and the blackberries, the pie and the two kinds of cake.

"What on earth do you mean goin'

on so queer?" said she, in a hesitating and somewhat conciliatory voice.

"I mean just what I said. That tree is a blessin' to me, it's company, and I think it's the handsomest tree any- wheres around. That's what I meant, and if you want to take me up for it, you can."

The cousin hesitated. She further reflected that she had in her solitary house no bread at all; she had not baked for two days. She would have to make a fire and bake biscuits in all that burning heat, and she had no cake nor berries. In fact, there was nothing whatever in her larder, except two cold potatoes, and a summer - squash pie, which she suspected was sour. She wanted to bury the hatchet, she wanted to stay, but her slow blood was up. All her strength of character lay in inertia.

One inertia of acquiescence was over, the other of dissent was triumphant. She could scarcely yield for all the bread and blackberries and cake. She shut up her fan with a clap.

"That fan was Marah's," said Sarah, meaningly, with a glance of reproach and indignation.

"I know it was Marah's," returned the cousin, rising with a jerk. "I know it was Marah's. 'Most everything I've got was hers, and I know that too. I ought to know it; I've been twitted about it times enough. If you think I ain't careful enough with her things, you can take them back again. If presents ain't mine after they've been give me, I don't want 'em."

The cousin went out of the room with a flounce of her purple muslin skirts. She passed into Sarah's little room where her cape and bonnet lay carefully placed on the snowy hill of the feather bed. She put them on, snatched up her green silk parasol, and passed through the sitting-room to the front entry.

"If you are a mind to go off mad, for such a thing as that, you can," said Sarah, rocking violently.

"You can feel just the way you want to," returned the cousin, with a sniff, "but you can't expect anybody with a mite of common-sense to fall in with such crazy ideas." She was out of the room and the house then with a switch, and speeding down the road with the green parasol bobbing overhead.

Sarah gave a sigh; she stared after her cousin's retreating form, then at the poplar-tree, and nodded as in confirmation of some resolution within her own mind. Presently she got up, looked on the table, then on the bed and bureau in the bedroom. The cousin had taken the fan.

Sarah returned to her chair, and sat fanning herself absent-mindedly. She gazed out at the yard and the poplar-tree. She had not resumed her wonted expression; the shadow of the stately, concentrated tree seemed still over her. She held her faded blond head stiff and high, her pale-blue eyes were steady, her chin firm above the lace ruffle at her throat. But there was sorrow in her heart. She was a creature of as strong race-ties as the tree. All her kin were dear to her, and the cousin had been the dearest after the death of her sister. She felt as if part of herself had been cut away, leaving a bitter ache of vacancy, and yet a proud self-sufficiency

"THE COUSIN CAUGHT HER BREATH WITH AN AUDIBLE
GASP"

was over her. She could exist and hold her head high in the world without her kindred, as well as the poplar. When it was tea-time she did not stir. She forgot. She did not rouse herself until the meeting-bell began to ring. Then she rose hurriedly, put on her bonnet and cape, and hastened down the road. When she came in sight of the church, with its open vestry windows, whence floated already singing voices, for she was somewhat late, she saw the cousin coming from the opposite direction. The two met at the vestry door, but neither spoke. They entered side by side; Sarah seated herself, and the cousin passed to the seat in front of her. The congregation, who were singing "Sweet Hour of Prayer," stared. There was quite a general turning of heads. Everybody seemed to notice

that Sarah Dunn and her cousin Sarah
Dunn were sitting in separate settees.
Sarah opened her hymn-book and held
it before her face. The cousin sang in
a shrill tremolo. Sarah hesitated a moment, then she struck in and sang louder.
Her voice was truer and better. Both
had sung in the choir when young.

The singing ceased. The minister,
who was old, offered prayer, and then
requested a brother to make remarks,
then another to offer prayer. Prayer
and remarks alike were made in a low,
inarticulate drone. Above it sounded
the rustle of the trees outside in a rising
wind, and the shrill reiteration of the
locusts invisible in their tumult of sound.
Sarah Dunn, sitting fanning, listening,
yet scarcely comprehending the human
speech any more than she comprehended
the voices of the summer night outside,

kept her eyes fastened on the straining surface of gray hair surmounted by the tiny black triangle of her cousin's bonnet. Now and then she gazed instead at the narrow black shoulders beneath. There was something rather pitiful as well as uncompromising about those narrow shoulders, suggesting as they did the narrowness of the life-path through which they moved, and also the stiff-neckedness in petty ends, if any, of their owner; but Sarah did not comprehend that. They were for her simply her cousin's shoulders, the cousin who had taken exception to her small assertion of her own individuality, and they bore for her an expression of arbitrary criticism as marked as if they had been the cousin's face. She felt an animosity distinctly vindictive towards the shoulders; she had an impulse to push and crowd in her own. The cousin sat fanning herself quite violently. Presently a short lock of hair on Sarah's forehead became disengaged from the rest, and blew wildly in the wind from the fan. Sarah put it back with an impatient motion, but it flew out again. Then Sarah shut up her own fan, and sat in stern resignation, holding to the recreant lock of hair to keep it in place, while the wind from the cousin's fan continued to smite her in the face. Sarah did not fan herself until the cousin laid down her fan for a moment, then she resumed hers with an angry sigh. When the cousin opened her fan again, Sarah dropped hers in her lap, and sat with one hand pressed against her hair, with an expression of bitter long-suffering drawing down the corners of her mouth.

# THE LOMBARDY POPLAR

After the service was over Sarah rose promptly and went out, almost crowding before the others in her effort to gain the door before her cousin. The cousin did the same; thus each defeated her own ends, and the two passed through the door shoulder to shoulder. Once out in the night air, they separated speedily, and each went her way to her solitary home.

Sarah, when she reached her house, stopped beside the poplar - tree and stood gazing up at its shaft of solitary vernal majesty. Its outlines were softened in the dim light. Sarah thought of the "pillar of cloud" in the Old Testament. As she gazed the feeling of righteous and justified indignation against the other Sarah Dunn grew and strengthened. She looked at the Lombardy poplar, one of a large race of trees,

159

all with similar characteristics which determined kinship, yet here was this tree as separate and marked among its kind as if of another name and family. She could see from where she stood the pale tremulousness of a silver poplar in the corner of the next yard. "Them trees is both poplars," she reflected, "but each of 'em is its own tree." Then she reasoned by analogy. "There ain't any reason why if Sarah Dunn and I are both Dunns, and look alike, we should be just alike." She shook her head fiercely. "I ain't goin' to be Sarah Dunn, and she needn't try to make me," said she, quite aloud. Then she went into the house, and left the Lombardy poplar alone in the dark summer night.

It was not long before people began to talk about the quarrel between the two Sarah Dunns. Sarah Dunn proper said nothing, but the cousin told her story right and left: how Sarah had talked as if she didn't have common-sense, putting an old, stiff popple-tree on a par with the folks she'd lost, and she, the cousin, had told her she didn't have common-sense, and then Sarah had ordered her out of her house, and wouldn't speak to her comin' out of meetin'. People began to look askance at Sarah Dunn, but she was quite unaware of it. She had formed her own plan of action, and was engaged in carrying it out. The day succeeding that of the dispute with the cousin was the hottest of a hot trio, memorable long after in that vicinity, but Sarah dressed herself in one of her cool old muslins, took her parasol and fan, and started to walk to Atkins, five miles distant, where all the stores were. She had to pass the cousin's house. The cousin, peering between the slats of a blind in the sitting - room, watched her pass, and wondered with angry curiosity where she could be going. She watched all the forenoon for her to return, but it was high noon before Sarah came in sight. She was walking at a good pace, her face was composed and unflushed. She held her head high, and walked past, her starched white petticoat rattling and her purple muslin held up daintily in front, but trailing in the back in a cloud of dust. Her white-stockinged ankles and black cloth shoes were quite visible as she advanced, stepping swiftly and precisely. She had a number of large parcels pressed closely to her sides under her arms and dangling by the strings from her hands. The cousin wondered unhappily what she had bought in Atkins. Sarah, passing, knew that she wondered, and was filled with childish triumph and delight. "I'd like to know what she'd say if she knew what I'd got," she said to herself.

The next morning the neighbors saw Annie Doane, who went out dressmaking by the day, enter Sarah Dunn's yard with her bag of patterns. It was the first time for years that she had been seen to enter there, for Sarah and Marah had worn their clothes with delicate care, and they had seldom needed replenishing, since the fashions had been ignored by them.

The neighbors wondered. They lay in wait for Annie Doane on her way home that night, but she was very close. They discovered nothing, and could not even guess with the wildest imagination what Sarah Dunn was having made. But the next Sunday a shimmer of red

silk and a toss of pink flowers were seen
at the Dunn gate, and Sarah Dunn,
clad in a gown of dark-red silk and a
bonnet tufted with pink roses, holding
aloft a red parasol, passed down the
street to meeting. No Dunn had ever
worn, within the memory of man, any
colors save purple and black and faded
green or drab, never any but purple or
white or black flowers in her bonnet.
No woman of half her years, and seldom
a young girl, was ever seen in the village clad in red. Even the old minister
hesitated a second in his discourse, and
recovered himself with a hem of em-
barrassment when Sarah entered the
meeting-house. She had waited until
the sermon was begun before she sailed
up the aisle. There were many of her
name in the church. The pale, small,
delicate faces in the neutral - colored

"THE LOMBARDY POPLAR - TREE STOOD IN ITS GREEN
MAJESTY BEFORE THE HOUSE"

bonnets stared at her as if a bird of another feather had gotten into their nest; but the cousin, who sat across the aisle from Sarah, caught her breath with an audible gasp.

After the service Sarah Dunn walked with her down the aisle, pressing close to her side. "Good-mornin'," said she, affably. The cousin in Marah's old black silk, which was matched by the one which Sarah would naturally have worn that Sunday, looked at her, and said, feebly, "Good - mornin'." There seemed no likeness whatever between the two women as they went down the aisle. Sarah was a Dunn apart. She held up her dress as she had seen young girls, drawing it tightly over her back and hips, elevating it on one side.

When they emerged from the meeting-house, Sarah spoke. "I should be happy to have you come over and spend the day to-morrow," said she, "and have a chicken dinner. I'm goin' to have the Plymouth Rock crower killed. I've got too many crowers. He'll weigh near five pounds, and I'm goin' to roast him."

"I'll be happy to come," replied the cousin, feebly. She was vanquished.

"And I'm goin' to give you my clothes like Marah's," said Sarah, calmly. "I'm goin' to dress different."

"Thank you," said the cousin.

"I'll have dinner ready about twelve. I want it early, so as to get it out of the way," said Sarah.

"I'll be there in time," said the cousin.

Then they went their ways. Sarah, when she reached home, paused at the front gate, and stood gazing up at the

poplar.   Then she nodded affirmatively
and entered the house, and the door
closed after her in her red silk dress.
And the Lombardy poplar - tree stood
in its green majesty before the house,
and its shadow lengthened athwart the
yard to the very walls.

The
APPLE-TREE

# THE APPLE-TREE

SAM MADDOX'S house was like a glaring blot on the tidy New England landscape, for the very landscape had been made to bear evidence to the character of the dwellers upon the soil. There was no wealth in the village, there was even poverty, but everywhere thrift and making the most of little, bringing out of humble possessions the very utmost that was in them for beauty and utility. When a house was scarcely larger than a child's toy it was white-painted and green-blinded, with windows shining like jewels; when there was only a little patch of yard, it was gay with flowers or velvet-smooth with grass; before it was a white fence or a trim green hedge, outside was a row of carefully tended trees. But Sam Maddox's house, unpainted since it was built, and that was nearly a hundred years since, sagging as to its roof and its sills, with a scant and ragged allowance of glass in the windows, with the sordid waste of poverty in shameless evidence around it on all sides, stood in a glaring expanse of raw soil, growing only a few clumps of burdocks, and marked in every direction with the sprawling tracks of omnipresent hens. In the first hot days of May this yard before Sam Maddox's house was a horror, actually provocative of physical discomfort to a sensitive observer. The sun lay on the

THE APPLE-TREE

front of the Maddox house and its yard
all day; every detail of squalor, so extreme that it reached the limit of de-
cency, was evident.  Passers-by turned
aside; even the sweet spring air was con-
taminated to their fancy; for it was not
in reality; it was only that the insult to
one sense seemed to imply an insult
to another.  In reality the air was
honey-sweet; for there was no crying
evil of uncleanliness about the place,
and in the midst of the yard was a whole
bouquet of spring.  That was the one
redemption of it all.  Often one, after
looking away, unless he was carping to
stiff - neckedness, would glance back-
ward, and the sight of the apple-tree
would serve as a solace to his very soul,
and beauty and the hope of the resur-
rection would vanquish squalor and the
despair of humanity.  There was never

173

a more beautiful apple-tree; majestic
with age, it yet had all the freshness of
youth and its perfection.   Not one dead
branch was there on the tree, not one
missing from its fair symmetry.   The
blooming spread of it was even to the
four winds; it described a perfect circle
of wonderful bloom.   The blossoms of
this apple-tree were unusually rosy—
they were as deep as roses, but with
shadows of pearl — and the fragrance
of them was exhaustless.   The whole
tree seemed to pant, and sing, and
shout with perfume; it seemed to call
even more loudly than the robins that
lived in its boughs.   The tree was
utter perfection, and a triumph over
all around it.

On the day in the month of May when
the tree was at its best, Sam Maddox
sat in the doorway, and his wife Ade-

line rocked back and forward past the open window. A baby wailed in her lap; she held a cheap novel over its head and read peacefully, undisturbed. Four more children pervaded the yard, their scanty little garments earth-stained, their faces and hands and legs and feet earth-stained. They had become in a certain sense a part of the soil, as much as the weeds and flowers of the spring. Their bare toes clung to the warm, kindly earth with caressing instinct; they grubbed in it tenderly with little, clinging hands; they fairly burrowed in it, in soft, sunny nests, like the hens. They made small, inarticulate noises, indicative of extreme comfort and satisfaction, like young which are nursed and coddled to their fill. There was very little strife and dissension among the Maddox children

in spite of their ill - repute and general
poverty and wretchedness. The Maddoxes were pariahs, suspected of all
sorts of minor iniquities, but in reality
they were a gentle, docile tribe, whose
gentleness and docility were the causes
of most of their failures of life. Sam
Maddox and his brood, lacking that of
comfort and necessaries which they saw
their neighbors possess, never thought of
complaining or grasping for the sweets
on the boughs behind their wall of fate.
They settled back unquestioningly on
the soft side of their poverty, and
slept, and smiled, and were not un-
happy.

Over across the road Mrs. Sarah
Blake cleaned house. She was small
and weak - muscled in spite of her life
of strenuous toil, which had bent her
narrow back and knotted her tiny

hands without strengthening them. She staggered out into the hot May sunlight with a great feather - bed, tugging it with a grip of desperation on the slack of one end. She dumped it into the midst of the green expanse of her front yard, between a tossing snowball bush and a syringa on one side and a strip of lilies-of-the-valley on the other; then she beat it with half-futile fury, assailing it like a live thing with a cane which her husband had used to walk abroad the year she was married, half a century ago. Sarah Blake was an old woman, although she had never confessed it, even to herself. Her two children were dead long ago, after they were women grown. There was no one except herself and husband, and Edison Blake was much older than she, stronger of body, though with less vigor of mind.

All the morning she had been striving in vain to whip up old Edison to the point of enthusiasm in house-cleaning. He was lukewarm, not openly rebellious, timid, but covertly dissenting. Whenever her back was turned, and she presumably out of hearing, old Edison, who had been considered unregenerate in his youth, would say something under his breath, and then glance apprehensively around, and then chuckle with defiance.

Once his wife heard him. She had left him meekly, to all appearances, cleaning the parlor windows. The old man was laboriously wiping off the panes with a cloth dipped in kerosene, the fumes of which were in his nostrils; he abominated kerosene. He was stout, and his fat, pink face was beaded with perspiration. He pulled his collar off with a jerk, then he said something with force. That time his wife heard him. She had not gone so far as he thought. She had come in for a clean little broom to sweep the feather-bed, after whipping it with the cane. "What did I hear you say, Edison Blake?" she demanded. She eyed him like an accusing conscience. Old Edison gave her one sidelong glance, then he turned to the window; he cleaned vigorously; he cocked his head on one side, busily, to see if a streak remained athwart the sunlight. "You needn't pretend you don't hear, and it wa'n't nothin', Edison Blake," said his wife Sarah. "I know you said something you didn't want me to hear, and now I want to know what it was."

"What you want to hear for, if it's somethin' you think wa'n't right?" inquired old Edison, with a feeble growl of self-assertion.

"I want to know," said she, ignoring the point of his remark.

"I didn't say much of anything," he hedged.

"What did you say, Edison Blake?"

"I said goll durn it, then, if you want to know," burst forth old Edison, with the fury of desperation.

"Edison Blake, I don't see what you think is goin' to become of you."

Old Edison was meek and always in a state of chronic intimidation by his wife, but all things have a bay. Old Edison could find his. He did now. He faced his wife Sarah. "It ain't likely, whatever is goin' to become of me, I'm goin' where there's house-cleanin', anyhow!" said he.

"You'll go where there's somethin' worse than house-cleanin'."

"It 'll have to be pooty goll durned bad to be any worse," said old Edison.

He looked steadily at his wife. She yielded, beaten by masculine assertion. She essayed one stony look of reproof, but her pale - blue eyes fell before the old man's, full of shrewd malice and quizzical triumph. She tossed her head and went out with her limp calico skirt lashing her thin ankles in a gust of spring wind. "When you get that winder finished you can come out an' help me shake the braided mat," she called back. She knew that would depress the victor, for she was merciless and miraculously untiring when it came to shaking a mat; she would not release the sufferer at the other end until not an atom of dust clouded the air. This time, however, fate, although an untoward one, interposed. Old Edison stepped in a chair to facilitate the process of cleaning the upper panes of the window, and the chair, dating back to the period of his wife's mother, and having seen better days as to its cane seat, and the old man being heavy, succumbed, and old Edison came with a jolt through to the floor. The thud brought in his wife Sarah, pale and gasping. When she saw her husband standing there in the wreck of the chair she stared a moment, then she spoke. Old Edison was holding to his head in a dazed fashion, not offering to move. "Now you've gone an' done it, Edison Blake!" said she.

"It give way all of a sudden an' let me through, Sarah," said old Edison, feebly.

"'NOW YOU'VE GONE AN' DONE IT, EDISON BLAKE!'"

"Didn't you know better than to stand up in one of them cane - seat chairs, heavy as you be?"

"I didn't know but it would bear me, Sarah!"

"Of course it wouldn't bear you. One of them nice cane-seat chairs that mother had when she was married! I'd ruther have given five dollar than had it happen."

"I'm dretful sorry, Sarah."

"I think you'd better be. Why don't you git out, an' not stand there starin' and hangin' onto your head?"

"My head is kind of dizzy, I guess, Sarah. I can't seem to see jest straight. I come down pooty hefty, I guess."

"You didn't come down on your head, did you? Looks to me as if you'd landed on your feet. That nice chair!"

"Yes, I s'pose I did land on my feet,

Sarah, but it ain't them that's hurt, but my head feels pooty bad, I guess."

There was, directly, no doubt that it did. Old Edison turned a ghastly, appealing face towards his wife, who promptly advanced, scolding the while, and strove to extricate him from the broken chair. But that was beyond her strength, and old Edison was unable to help himself, although he was not unconscious. He continued to make feebly deprecatory remarks as he failed to respond to his wife's futile efforts.

Finally Sarah Blake made an impatient exclamation. "Well, I ain't goin' to work this way for nothin' any longer," said she. Then she was gone, not heeding the weak inquiry as to what she was going to do which her husband sent after her.

Straight across the road she raced,

with skirts and apron flying to the wind like sails, making pitiless revelations of ascetic anatomy. Straight up to Sam Maddox in his peaceful leisure on the front doorstep she went. "Edison has fell and hurt himself, gone through one of the cane-seat chairs my mother had when she was married," she said, in an accusing tone, "an' he's stuck there in it, and I want you to come right over and git him out. I can't lift him, and he won't help himself one mite."

Sam Maddox raised his shaggy, blond head, and brought his pleasant blue eyes and pleasanter gaping mouth to bear upon her.

"Hey?" he said, inquiringly, with a long, husky drawl.

Sarah Blake repeated the burden of her speech with furious emphasis.

"You want me to come over and help git him out?" said Sam Maddox. Adeline Maddox had come to the door, and the small baby in her arms was uttering wails of feeble querulousness unheeded.

"Yes, I do want somebody to come over an' git him out," said Sarah Blake. "I can't lift him, an' he'll stan' there till doomsday, for all he'll help himself."

"Is he hurt?" inquired Sam Maddox, with some interest.

"Says his head's kind of dizzy; he looks kinder pale. I s'pose he come down pretty hard. He went right through the seat of that chair, an' the cane-seat wa'n't broke a mite before."

"I'll come right along," said Sam Maddox, and straightway rose with

186

loose sprawls of ungainly limbs. He seemed a kindly and ineffectual giant when he stood up; he had doubled up an enormous length of limb in his sitting posture.

Sam Maddox followed, with long, languid strides, Sarah Blake, who hopped on before him, like a nervous bird, across the street. After them streamed the Maddox children, a white-headed, earth - stained troop; in the rear of all came Adeline Maddox, her paper novel fluttering, the small baby wailing, her yellow hair flying in strings.

"There ain't no need of the whole family," Sarah Blake called out sharply once, but they came on smilingly.

Poor old Edison Blake was sitting on the ragged edge of the broken chair when they arrived. "I swun!" said

Sam Maddox, when he caught sight of him.

He lifted him out bodily and laid him on the lounge, and Sarah got the camphor-bottle.

She was not in the least alarmed. "He come down pretty hard, and his head wa'n't never very strong," she said. She bathed his forehead with the camphor with hard strokes, she got it in his eyes, and she pushed back his hair remorselessly. "Keep still. I'm goin' to see to it that you git enough camphor to do some good," said she, firmly, when old Edison pushed her hand away from his smarting eyes.

"You're gitting of it in my eyes, Sarah," he remonstrated, meekly. All his spirit was gone, between the hurt to the chair and himself.

"You keep still," said she, and old

Edison screwed his eyes tightly together. His color was fast returning.
He was evidently not much the worse,
but he groaned when his wife inquired
how he felt now.

"Seems to me he'd better keep still
awhile," said Sam Maddox, looking at
him compassionately. "Seems to me
he hadn't better clean winders till he's
rested a little whilst."

"We've got somethin' to do beside
rest over here," replied Sarah Blake,
with unmistakable emphasis. Sam Maddox smiled, and Adeline smiled foolish-
ly and sweetly. They appreciated the
sarcasm, and took it amiably.

However, old Edison groaned again,
and Sarah left him in peace on the
lounge, when the Maddoxes streamed
homeward across the street, and she
returned to the yard to resume her

struggle with the feather-bed and the mats.

She was somewhat at a loss when it came to the braided mat which belonged in the sitting-room. It was a large mat, and very heavy. She strove to lift it; she could scarcely do that. She strove to shake it; as well try to shake the side of the house. She eyed it as if it were some refractory animal. The negative opposition of inanimate things always filled this small, intense woman with fury. She let the mat slide to the ground; she gave a weary and angry sigh. Then she looked across the street. There sat Sam Maddox on his doorstep, lazily regarding her. He had certainly seen her helpless effort to shake the braided mat. She stood eying him for one minute. Then across the street she marched.

"THERE SAT SAM MADDOX ON HIS DOORSTEP"

She stood before Sam Maddox, electric, compelling, this small, delicate old woman before this great, lumbering giant of a man.

"Sam Maddox, I'd like to know what you mean?" said she.

He stared at her. "Hey?" he said.

"I'd like to know what you think of yourself?"

"Hey?"

"I'd like to know what you think of yourself? You heard what I said the first time. If you was my son, I'd cure you of sayin' 'hey,' if I killed you. If you hear, why don't you hear? You are too lazy to sense things even, unless somebody else drives 'em into your head to save you the trouble of takin' 'em in. I'd like to know what you think of yourself?"

"I dun'no'," said Sam Maddox.

"I guess you don't know. If you did know, you wouldn't keep your settin' long. 'Ain't you been lookin' over the road at me tryin' to shake that great mat all alone, and you doin' nothin'?"

Sam Maddox hitched. His wife, Adeline, with the baby, came slowly to the front; the earth-stained children gathered round.

"What did you s'pose I was goin' to do?" queried Sarah Blake.

Sam Maddox looked at her with the perplexed stare of a good-natured dog trying with the limitations of his doghood to comprehend a problem of humanity; then he murmured feebly again that he didn't know.

"And me with my husband laid up with falling through one of my mother's nice cane-seat chairs that she had when

she was married!" said Sarah Blake,
further.

Adeline, who was weakly emotional,
wiped her eyes. Sam Maddox, feeling it
incumbent upon him to make some response, and finding speech inadequate,
grunted.

"Well, ain't you goin' to do nothin'
but sit there and stare?" demanded Sarah Blake, with a sort of cold fury.

Sam Maddox rose and shuffled before
her, as if essaying a dance.

"For the land's sake! 'ain't you got
any gumption, no snap at all? Be you
goin' to sit there an' see me tryin' to
shake that great, heavy mat, an' never
offer to raise a finger?"

"Do go over there an' help her shake
her mat, Sam," sniffed Adeline.

A look of joyous relief overspread Sam
Maddox's perplexed face. He start-

ed with perfect assent. "Sartain," he drawled—"sartain."

"I'll make it wuth your while," said Sarah Blake.

Sam stopped and eyed her doubtfully.

"What?" said he.

"I'll see to it you're paid for it."

Sam settled loosely on to the doorstep again; a look of evanescent firmness overspread his face.

"Ain't you comin'?"

"I ain't workin'," said Sam Maddox.

"Mebbe you think we can't pay enough. I guess we can pay as much as your work is wuth, Sam Maddox. We ain't in the poor-house yet."

"I ain't workin'."

"He means he don't do no work for money. Don't you, Sam?" inquired Adeline, tearfully. The baby whimpered, and she dandled it with no enthusiasm.

"He won't work for pay?" inquired Sarah Blake, dazedly.

"I don't shake mats for old women for no pay," said Sam Maddox, with who could tell what species of inborn pride or generosity?

"You mean you'd rather come for nothin'?"

Sam nodded obstinately.

"You think we ain't able to pay you?" asked Sarah, jealously.

"Dun'no', and don't care."

"You mean you just won't?"

Sam nodded.

"Why don't you come, then, an' not keep me standin' here all day? I want to git that settin'-room cleaned, if I can, to-day."

Sam rose again, and slouched across

the road in the wake of the little, vociferous, indefatigable woman. He looked, this great, loosely built, ineffectual, blond giant of a man, the very antipode to the woman snapping with her overplus of energy, as she led the way to the scene of labor. He might have been an inhabitant of another planet.

Now, indeed, came a time of trial to Sam Maddox. From where he toiled, in the Blake yard, he could see, like a vision of a lost paradise, his old comfortable door-step, the door-post which leaned luxuriously to his back, the warm sunlight which overspread the whole place like a sea of blessing. The clamor of the happy children playing about with an incessant enjoyment of youth and life was as pleasant to him as the hum of bees. Adeline rocked ever back and forth past the window with an inertia of peace, and the great apple-tree perfumed and irradiated the whole. Sam Maddox glanced scornfully at the small, reluctant pear-tree in the Blake yard.

"What be you a-lookin' at?" inquired Sarah Blake from the other end of the braided mat. "Shake it this way."

"Your pear-tree don't amount to much, does it?" said Sam Maddox.

"No, it don't, and they're winter pears on that tree, too. They last till long after Thanksgivin'. I always make sauce of 'em an' have 'em for supper Thanksgivin' night. We don't want much after turkey dinner, an' a little of that pear-sauce used to go jest right. I dun'no' what ails that tree. He trimmed it up real nice, too."

"Mebbe he trimmed it too much."

"No, he didn't. I ain't goin' to have old, dead branches or spindlin' ones that don't amount to much on a tree in my yard. I believe in keeping trees nice an' neat as well as houses."

"'Ain't never tetched my apple-tree," observed Sam Maddox, with unusual pride.

Sarah sniffed. "Well, I suppose the Lord looks out for trees, the same as he does for folks, when they 'ain't got anybody else," said she.

"It's a pretty handsome tree," said Sam Maddox, ignoring the sarcasm.

"I don't care nothin' about the looks of a tree so long as it has good apples. I want apples to last all winter, good, sound ones. I want 'em for my Thanksgivin' pies. I feel thankful for apples like that, but I can't say as I do, if I say just what I think, for them early kinds."

"The apples on that tree would keep if we let 'em, I reckon," said Sam Maddox, "but we don't make pies nor sauce of 'em, and we eat 'em right up. They ain't quite so meller. The children are dreadful fond of them apples."

"I didn't s'pose you did make pies," said Sarah, and she sniffed.

"I never see blooms so pink as them," said the man, gazing with the expression of an artist at the tree.

"I don't care nothin' about blooms; it's apples I'm arter," said Sarah.

That was a red-letter day for old Edison Blake. He fell asleep on the sitting-room lounge, and when he awoke was fully aware that the dizziness in his head was gone. He felt guiltily that he ought to rise and resume his labor, but he could not resist the impulse to remain in his comfortable place a little longer. Sam Maddox passed the open window with a braided mat over his shoulder. Old Edison heard his wife's sharp voice of direction and admonition. "She's got Sam Maddox helpin' her," he reflected. He knew how small an opinion his wife had of Sam Maddox, he knew that he ought to rise, but he lay still. Pretty soon Sam entered the room for a brush. Old Edison lay with eyes wide open regarding him. Sam paused and stooped over him.

"Better?" he inquired.

Old Edison closed his eyes in affirmation.

"Dizzy feelin' gone?"

"'Bout."

Sam Maddox looked down at the aged, recumbent figure. "Look here," he said. He bent low and whispered sharply, "Don't you git up. You jest lay low. It's durned hard work, house-cleanin'; you're too old. You lay low. I'll stay round and help."

Old Edison looked at him with intensest gratitude; an expression of bliss overspread his face. He smiled the smile of a contented baby.

"Just go to sleep ag'in," said Sam Maddox.

Old Edison closed his eyes.

When Sam Maddox emerged from the house, Sarah Blake inquired how her husband was.

"Looks pretty slim to me," said Sam Maddox.

"Asleep?"

"His eyes was shut; looked as if he was. Seems to me he ought to keep pretty still."

"Guess he can keep still enough," said Sarah. Pretty soon she went in to peep at old Edison. He lay drawing long, even, whistling breaths. When she went out of the room he gazed after her from the corner of one cautious eye.

Sam Maddox worked all that beautiful May day for Sarah Blake. She was the hardest, and, in fact, the only task-mistress of life whom he had ever known. Sam had lived somehow without much work. He owned his poor house and lot and apple-tree. People who pitied the children of the irresponsible pair assisted them. Once in a while he went gunning and fishing. Somehow they lived and were happy. When Sam Maddox went home that night, the oldest girl had dug a mess of dandelions, and there was a parcel of cress from the bank of the brook.

Somehow there were a loaf of bread, and molasses, and tea. Sam had no idea how they were procured, but there they were. They all ate and were thankful. After supper, in the delicious cool of the day, Sam sat on the doorstep. Adeline put the baby to bed, then she came and sat by her husband's side, her elbows on her knees, her delicate chin in her hands, and her sharp, pretty face upturned towards the ineffable clear pallor of the sky. The children had subsided, and were grouped in a charming little cluster like a bunch of flowers in the yard under the apple-tree. And the apple-tree was a mystery of whiteness and ravishing fragrance. In the day it had been simply a magnificent apple-tree; when the shadows came, it was something more. Sam Maddox gazed at it, and the breath

of it came over his senses. He looked
across at the Blake house in its tidy
yard. There was a light in the sitting-
room, and a small figure bustled back
and forth incessantly past the window.
Now and then a larger, taller shape
lumbered before the light. There was
a sound of a hammer and a sharp
voice.

"Old Edison, he's had one day off,
anyhow," chuckled Sam Maddox. He
stretched his great limbs, which ached
with the unaccustomed strain of the
day's toil. He continued to gaze reflectively at the Blake house. "Dreadful clean over there," he murmured.

"S'pose so," assented Adeline, indifferently. There was an angelic expression in her face, upturned towards
the sky. Possibly her imagination,
from the slight stimulus of a third-rate

"'I DON'T SEE WHY WE 'AIN'T GOT THANKSGIVIN' ANY
TIME'"

novel, was making a leap out of her surroundings.

"Says she cleans house once a month from now till Thanksgivin', on account of the dust, an' the winders havin' to be open so much," said Sam Maddox.

"Lord!" said Adeline, indifferently.

"I shouldn't think they'd have any Thanksgivin' when they got to it, workin' so hard, an' fussin' all the time. I shouldn't."

Then Adeline looked with strong disapproval across at the Blake house. "Doggin' round all day," said she.

"That's so," assented Sam. "It's terrible hard work cleanin' house."

"What's the use? It gits dirty again," said Adeline.

"That's so." Sam looked again at the great apple-tree. "Mighty handsome tree," said he.

Adeline looked and smiled. Her face was really beautiful. "Real handsome," said she.

"I don't see no use in waitin' for Thanksgivin', fussin' and cleanin' an' cookin'. I don't see why we 'ain't got Thanksgivin' any time right along any time of year," said Sam, thoughtfully.

"That's so," said Adeline, nodding happily.

Sam gazed at her. "Seems as if you got better-lookin' than ever," he said. "You ain't tired, be you?"

"No; 'ain't done nothin' all day. You tired, Sam?"

"Sorter. Hard work cleanin' house."

"You can rest to-morrer."

Sam nodded, still with tender eyes on his wife's face.

The wind blew, and a wonderful breath of fragrance came from the apple-tree, and they inhaled it. "Lord, it's a dreadful pretty world, ain't it?" said Sam Maddox, and on his face was a light of unconscious praise.

"Yes, 'tis," said Adeline, and her face looked like her husband's.

The splendid apple-tree bloomed and sweetened, and the man and woman, in a certain sense, tasted and drank it until it became a part of themselves, and there was in the midst of the poverty and shiftlessness of the Maddox yard a great inflorescence of beauty for its redemption.

THE END